The Dream

...That Almost Lived

The Dream

...That Almost Lived

Upneet Grover

MP
MAHAVEER PUBLISHERS

Published by
MAHAVEER PUBLISHERS
4764/2A, 23-Ansari Road, Daryaganj
New Delhi – 110002
Ph. : 011 – 66629669–79–89
e-mail : mahaveerpublishers@gmail.com

First Edition : October 2012

The Dream ...That Almost Lived
ISBN : 9788183520287

This novel is entirely a work of fiction. Names, characters and incidents portrayed in it are the work of the author's imagination. Any resemblance to actual persons, living or dead, events or localities is entirely coincidental.

Distributed in India by
VAIBHAV BOOK SERVICE
e-mail : vaibhavbookservice@gmail.com

Distributed in Nepal by
BAJRANGBALI BOOK ENTERPRISES PVT. LTD.
Jyatha Mushyabahal, Ward No. 27, Kathmandu, Nepal
e-mail : bajrangbalibooks@gmail.com

Printed in India

Dedication

To my sister Ishu who believed
To my parents who still can't
To Hardik who encouraged
To Sai who mindlessly praised
To Prachita for making me read
To Aanandita for her edits
And to all my friends who tried to go through the unedited versions of the script just to make me feel happy

Acknowledgment

Ever nursed a childhood dream of being a doctor, an actor, IAS officer or a sportsperson? While your head makes a decision of its own to nod with a "Yes," it also recalls how passionate you felt about those inane pursuits, which were so special to you. As life trudged along and you realised that such things actually happen only in movies, you gave up, without even trying.

Having been one such dreamer myself, I write this novel for everyone who has ever nurtured a dream. A dream which once shone like a pearl, but then slowly faded into nothingness. This novel is a shot in the arm for those, who still would want to leave everything aside, just to have that one jab at glory. In this novel I present to you a no holds barred story of just another guy like you and me, who is so similar, yet so different.

Confessions of the Cricketer

You might or might not remember me, I don't blame you. Most of them don't.

This book is a narrative of my journey to become a cricketer. It isn't an autobiography as there have been fictional episodes added to it. That's because I wanted anonymity to be maintained, but the essence of this story is as true as it gets.

I thank Upneet, to have taken out his time and energy to write this book on my behalf and give words to the feelings of an obscure cricketer who once wasn't as obscure, and to give me an outlet for my thoughts and emotions that have been bottled up for a long time now.

Contents

Contents

CHAPTER 1
The Office

"Knowing yourself is the beginning of all wisdom."

— Aristotle

I jerked out of my ghastly nightmare; thanks to that asshole Nikhil, guffawing like a maniac at Vivek,who, it seemed, had spilled coffee over himself. It hadn't recurred for a long time now – I mean - the nightmare. Unbelievably, each moment of the incident that triggered the nightmare was still crystal- clear in my memory, even though it had happened 10 years ago. I can recall the moment in which I had lost my parents in the car accident, it would seem as though it happened only yesterday.

Back to reality. I see these software junkies all around me. They keep banging the daylights out of their hapless keyboards. The noise is incessant, broken only by the intermittent sniggers over an internal joke during one of the million coffee breaks. I sat desolate, in my own corner of the cubicle, rarely participating in any of these activities. I seldom did any work, never had coffee, and despised these jokes about insignificant office happenings. My loathing for office was known to all, including my project manager.

Information Technology never interested me, programming language I had never comprehended and why I had graduated as an engineer was a question as bemusing to me as much as the question - Why do people have so much coffee in office? Mostly in my own world, I usually daydreamed sitting in office.

"Hey it's lunch time, care to join me??" asked Simi, the prettiest girl in my project group. She wore a light blue salwar-kameez and stood at the entrance tomy cubicle with a hopeful smile across her face. In any other world, I would have fallen for her. But here, the fact that she was a little slow in the head, added to the strict law which my manager had laid down(which clearly stated not to be "overfriendly" with any member of the opposite sex in the project group), I never took a fancy to her.

To think of it again, to say Simi was the prettiest girl in my project group would be an understatement. Her flowing, perfectly trimmed hair which danced as she walked, her glossy lips which emitted wafts of fruity lip balm scents and her eyes which spoke more elegantly than her lips managed to, had a major chunk of the Infotech male employees fall head-over-heels in love with her.

"Nope, not really hungry, I'll eat later. You carry on," I said, cutting a sorry figure, although, I was indeed hungry. Somehow I liked dismissing her. There was a sadistic pleasure in showing off to everyone in office how I never cared, even though the best of the fairer sex invited me personally for lunch, an invitation for which most of the people in office would have given up their coffee for a whole week.

This was the sole way of asserting my presence in the project group –a group in which I was considered a lazy bum, a no-good employee just biding his time and getting straight D's in his performance appraisals, which, in fact, required enormous talent. Only the bottom-most 5%, in a company boasting of over 1 lakh employees, could manage that. Not surprisingly, most of them were shown the exit door. When I would get this opportunity was what I wondered about all day.

It was two o' clock and the employees at the client site had just started entering the office in Belgium. The lights against their names on the office chat communicator were beginning to go green indicating that they were now online. This was the scariest moment of the day for me because it was usually this time when work picked up pace, and it made me pray every single day for a power cut. If only such things happened in the biggest IT firm of the country!

My inbox started filling at a rate that seemed to match my heartbeat and eventually, surpassed it by much. All of my previous day's work had either been rubbished or so many corrections had been pointed out that I figured doing it all over again would save me more time.

With my head cupped in my hands, I sat wondering when I would escape this misery. It was then that my cell phone vibrated against the desk.

"Hey baby, was sup? Tea in 10?" Sonali had messaged. Sonali was a tall, slim woman with perfect curves and a face which bordered precariously on bewitching. She had an air of subtle naughtiness, something that had attracted me the very first minute I had set my eyes on her at Infotech Ltd. A few dates later, she and I decided to give our liking for each other a shot and transformed it into a relationship.

"How about in 5?" I texted back. Anything to run away from this god forsaken place, I thought.

"What shit all day. I haven't done anything worthwhile since morning and it's already 4 o'clock. Read the newspaper twice, memorised Cricinfo's articles and chatted with half the list on my communicator," I yapped, sipping on my chocolate milk shake.

"You are so darn cute!!" she said, apparently finding my rant adorable.

"I've had a really hard day, two client calls and so much work. I won't be back before 9 today," she stated, sitting in a khakhi green shirt which was amazingly unwrinkled for four o'clock in the evening. By this time, half my shirt was untucked and crumpled beyond recognition and had started to look like a 'Shyam and Tailors' shirt rather than the 'Park Avenue' it originally started out as. The squirming and shifting all day long in my office chair was to be blamed.

"C'mon Simi, today is Friday, we were going out! Remember freshly brewed beer?" I exclaimed, both complaining and trying to entice her strategically, assuming it would work.

"Sorry baby, can't we go tomorrow?" she asked, with furrowed brows. "Why on earth was she so damn sincere," I thought. She was an exact opposite to me, when it came to work ethics. Arriving at the office at sharp nine, working well beyond the mandatory work hours and a couple of 'best employee,' and 'most valuable player' awards made her what would be called a model employee. The theory that opposites attract, was at its best demonstration in our case.

"Whatever! Go to hell." I stood up and gulped the last of my milkshake and left with the sandwich in hand. I've never liked wasting perfectly good food.

She called me, probably asking me to come back, but I cancelled the call, trotting away, searching for ideas of how to spend my empty Friday evening. Back at my cubicle, the horrifying pings had packed up the screen, all instructing me to do one task or another, all of which I loathed equally, without any bias. The clock ticked slowly, like a clueless goat on a highway. Finally, after what felt like an eternity, it somehow managed to chime 6. The female half of the project team had already started leaving, as was the norm for them. Some had personal reasons; some were going early just that one (billionth) time and the others didn't even need to cite a reason for leaving an hour earlier than the mandatory nine hours.

Anyhow, I was the last person to judge them. I had consistently clocked seven and a half hours and had made so many trips to the HR department that I could see "Screw you! Not again!" written all over my HR representative's face whenever I visited her.

Thanks to my deep- rooted male ego, out of no cogent logic, I had somehow convinced myself that the HR rep. had started liking me, because sometimes she called me for a hearing even though I had been a better employee than last time. My not meeting the'company's benchmark for professional excellence' somehow, was her favourite excuse for seeing me. So much for a bunch of losers wasting their lives in a computer junkyard, I would think, smiling to myself.

At one point, I was sure that she indeed had fallen for me, and consequently I asked her out for coffee. She looked at me with such large repulsion-laden eyes, that I was afraid her eyeballs would fall out of their sockets into the coffee mug. She was aghast at my audacity, which again, I initially mistook for a pleasant surprise on her part about the fact that a good-looking lad like me had asked her out.

It turned out, it was the other way round and she warned me never to go for it again or else she'd book me under some shady sexual harassment code of the company. I shrugged and left the room, after asking her to "get a life," with another poor code of conduct letter. No wonder I was getting straight D's.

"Hey, someone is planning on being the CEO soon," my cubicle mates would start teasing me, if I ever stayed on till 6:15.

I used to get the drift and soon walked out, smiling and mumbling profanities at them. They too smirked back. Basically, no one cared, neither them nor me. It was just a game for them and an even funnier one for me.

❖ ❖ ❖

That evening I went to a friend's place and got drunk; nothing special, just another Friday evening. Saturday mornings were not easy, though, getting up and 'trying' to have fun, because the daunting Monday always weighed on my mind.

I tried a little too hard sometimes, so much so that I occasionally wondered whether it was actually worth it to expend so much effort for having fun. Getting up at 9:00 a.m. to watch a movie, stuffing myself with outside food all day, and catching up on another movie in the evening sure wasn't as much fun as it sounded.

After much deliberation and office hearsay, I had decided that my exit strategy from Infotech would be an MBA degree. I hardly ever worked or met any office deadlines, but my consistently poor mock scores for the MBA degree I wanted to pursue pushed me into thinking that if I wouldn't be able to get into an MBA college the same year and if at the same time, I got a kick on my posterior from the HR department, then what would become of me?

The only time in the day when I felt at peace with myself was when I was pumping those plates of iron in the gym after office hours. Someone aptly said that the iron never lies... I believed in that statement more than anything else. I was so disciplined about my gymming, that I sometimes shocked myself. No matter how tired I was, I would visit the gym, do my scheduled set of exercises and only then come back home. This routine was only seldom broken, that is, when Sonali would coax me to an evening outing followed by dinner and 'dessert' at her place. The last part was the only reason I'd leave the gym.

"One more! Don't be such a wuss," Hardik, my best friend at my workplace and otherwise, challenged me, while I was benching 200 pounds and was on my last rep. I obliged nonetheless, but almost ended up having my head ripped off as the weight was way too much for my still developing, but otherwise lean pectoral muscles, when Hardik acted as a perfect spotter and saved me.

"Screw you ass hole, don't try and motivate me next time, I'll hurt myself someday!" I cried, my throat hoarse from the exertion.

"Bloody sham of a bodybuilder," he taunted me, and chuckled as he placed his towel on the bench for his turn.

He'd bench half as much as I did, but justified it by attributing this to the fact that he weighed a 'measly' 60 kgs as compared to my 80 kgs.

"If only you'd bench half as well as you bark," I taunted back as he struggled with his 120 pounds. I usually spotted his benching weight with one hand and always counted lower repetitions than he had actually done, to get his irritation levels higher.

Hardik was a gregarious guy, chirpier than a girl. He had the uncanny knack of getting me into a good mood whenever I was tense. His face was triangular in shape, with short, cropped golden hair making it appear as if he was straight out of a cartoon series. He had a good body though, he was ripped at the arms and chest and I envied him for that. I never praised him though, lest he'd rub it in my face with every opportunity he would've got.

After the workout and shower, we were contemplating our further plan of action when he asked, "How about some beer at Toons?"

"No way! I am not ruining my workout. Do you know alcohol after a workout negates all its positive effects?" I retorted, throwing a piece of trivia at him, something I'd remembered after the countless hours spent reading about weight training during office hours.

"Ah! Mr. Arnold Schwarzenegger speaks again. Don't gimme that shit. What does a muscle know what I eat? It could be an egg or ethanol!" he retorted.

I was almost ready to unleash my repertoire of bodybuilding knowledge at him when I thought the better of it and stopped.

"Ok!! Let's go. Can I call Sonali, if you don't mind?" I asked.

"Oh hell, I mind! You two will begin whispering sweet nothings and start smiling and looking at each other for no god damned reason. Even though it is a reason good enough to bang my head on the table repeatedly, all evening long. So, in short, NO!" he roared.

"Ok, man! Easy!" I said, trying to calm him down. Deep down inside, I understood how insanely boring it was to go out with a dating couple and be the odd one out. Always looking for a moment for you to go take a squirt, or go get the drinks, or for that matter, just leave the table so that they can say the same thing to each other they've said all day on messages and calls.

Toons was an awesome place. Cheap beer, delicious food, hep crowd. The songs that were played were a part of my shallow knowledge of English numbers, enabling me to hum/head bang along. The girls there were good-looking enough so that even if there was nothing to talk about, covert staring at them would just about suffice for the evening. To top it all off, there were the sports channels, both cricket and football, depending upon which of the two had a more important event going on. I really did not care about football. Cricket, though, I loved.

That day there was an India v/s Australia T20 match lined up, which had somehow slipped both our minds. An IT job does that to you. Anyhow, Toons was packed when we entered, and after forty-five minutes of ogling at chilled beer and scantily clad females, we got a table for two.

"Hey, this seems like a date!" Hardik said, trying to rub me the wrong way.

"Which dickhead would get a date to this place with such deafeningly loud music, beer and cricket, all three of which girls hate?" I countered, trying to prove my point, but then I shut up and I realised how this was perfect for a gay date. Only that it was not one.

"Two Budweisers and peanuts!" I ordered.

Our love for cricket was equal in passion but I kicked his ass when it came to chucking statistics at each other. Post-game analysis was an activity where we almost came to dirty name-calling and threw the obscenities freely at each other just to give more gravity to our point of view.

We sometimes discuss certain technicalities too. We'd correct Sachin's cover drive, Sehwag's slog and Warne's leg break in our deliberations. Something which someone else would burst out into laughter, on hearing .

"What an idiot this Sehwag is!! Bloody empty-headed asshole... literally and metaphorically," Hardik stated in an irritated voice after India's drubbing by Australia.

"Oh! So now at a strike rate of 150, he should also have an average of 50 in T20s?? He is a match winner, you loser!" I said, coming in to save my favourite player's stature.

"Why can't he do it? Yuvraj has a good strike rate and a good average, that's what good players are all about. Not empty-headed sloggers, you mother..." He stopped, controlling his emotions at just the right time.

"Haan, say it asshole!" I taunted.

After a dud moment, we both laughed and argued for another 2 hours, over 5 Budwiesers.

❖ ❖ ❖

My life continued, with Sonali and Hardik playing the most pivotal roles in it. My only good chance to escape this hell hole came nearer, i.e. my CAT exam. I realised that beer guzzling had to come down and so did my evening dates with Sonali. She was also preparing for the same exam and keeping this in mind, we made a plan. I would work till six in the office, beyond which was not humanely possible for me, and then I would leave for the gym. She would continue to work till seven or eight or till whenever her manager would leave, and then we would sit together in some third random person's cubicle to study together.

This was one bad idea. All we managed to do were to convey the same love-smitten whispers and murmurs, watch her blush and sneak in an odd kiss when everyone around, left. It went on for a week and when that Sunday's mock test turned out to be a disaster for both of us, we decided we'd do the same thing over, but in two separate cubicles which would be sufficiently faraway from each other, so that none of us could keep coming to the other every ten minutes.

It was a rainy Sunday with just two months left and hardly a few practice tests remaining.

"You know, this is the first time I'm scared. I just hope this time I cross the 98 percentile mark. Hardly two months left. If I don't do well, I'll lose all my confidence," I said, sounding morose as I spoke to Sonali while leaving for the test centre.

"Oh come on, you're damn intelligent. It's just that you screw up one section every single time. This time try and spend less time on Maths and more on the other two to get a balanced score," she explained tactfully. I must confess, it was a turn-on to see such a cute girl talk about such grave things in an even cuter manner.

I pulled her cheek and playfully said, "Ok baby!! A 99 percentile this time, just for you!"

A 71 was what I ended up with. The lesser time dedicated to Maths screwed me up completely since this was one section which kept my scores high. I learnt I was a hopeless case and should give up. But then, nightmares about spending my life in office flashed before my eyes and I realised giving up was not an option, and that I needed to work harder. The only question was, how?

"After such grueling hours in office, how can one study?" I growled at Hardik on the Monday after the horror mock test.

"You hardly study and you're no prodigy that you'll crack the test just sitting on your ass. You need more time, son," he explained, taking the paternal tone.

"And from where should I get that extra time, quit this job? Which gives me cash to have beer, buy adidas and eat butter chicken?" I said, stating all the things where the major chunk of my salary was spent.

"Who said you should quit? Sabbatical, my boy, sabbatical; or in simple terms, a sick leave. Do you know how many people get jaundice? Plus, if it's really bad, it can take up to two months to heal" he said, chuckling, and winked at me as he planted the seed in my mind.

CHAPTER 2

The CAT

"Genius is one percent inspiration and ninety-nine percent perspiration."

– Thomas Alva Edison

I packed my bags that very night and told Sonali that I'd be leaving for home in a day.

"What? Are you crazy? What does that mean? What if you are fired? What if you screw up CAT also? When are you planning to come back?" Sonali threw a whole string of questions at me, to which I merely replied, "I love you, and I'll be back soon."

She hung up and I didn't call back because she sounded like she was in a mood to blast me into smithereens. She would talk continuously for an hour with bursts of hysterical howling in between, to which I'd have just one answer, "I love you, yaar."

Later in the night when I felt that she would have calmed down, it still took me an hour to explain everything to her. I promised that I'd call her every day and that we'd chat every night. I also promised I'd not stare at Delhi girls and would definitely not visit any of my female friends during my 'supposed' studying stint at home. I kept all the promises except the staring at the hot girls' one. That was just too much, I wasn't GOD!

❖ ❖ ❖

"I am such an idiot!Why did I give you that stupid idea? Now I'll get so damn bored these two months. Have you thought who I'll go to the gym with?" Hardik complained, supposedly high on estrogen while dropping me to the airport.

"Relax, bhai. I'll be back in a month, right after CAT. Anyhow, I feel you need a break from the gym. You've become very bulky," I said, mocking at him.

"Oh, go away. When you come back, I'll be done with my six packs!" he retorted.

I wished him good luck with that and we waved casual good-byes to each other just like unemotional guys do, but I could still feel the pinch of leaving my best friend and the girl I love, for an exam which I was likely to mess up in a major way.

Home for me meant staying in a small, cozy house in West Delhi with my grandmother. Grandma was the only family I was left with...someone I could actually call family. When I was twelve, she had taken me home. This had been soon after the accident and I had been shell-shocked as a result. On the brink of eternal muteness, I was too stunned to understand what had happened. Had grandma not been there, well, I can't imagine what would have happened? For a 70-year old widow, she was a strong lady.

From whatever little pension she got and with no financial help from any of the relatives, she raised me single-handedly. In the ten years before that, I can't recall one instance where she raised her voice while talking to me and I always tried my best not to give her a reason to do so.

Having returned home for preparations, I had to pull up my socks and get down to it; which I did. The month and a half at home was the first time in the last two years that I felt I was actually doing something constructive. Application of my grey matter felt good after a brainless year of coding and building a façade of working at office. Here I was solving problems which, if done properly, would give me the license to claim my stature as one of the brightest brains in a country boasting over 1.2 billion people. 'No mean feat,' I thought.

I put in a lot of hours and consequently, the last three mock tests showed a drastic change in my scores. On the other hand, I kept my promise to Sonali and called her up regularly. I really missed her physical presence, her cute, never-ending stories about office happenings and the lunches in the Infotech canteen. I counted, the days, yearning to see her again.

❖ ❖ ❖

Then came D-day and I couldn't be more nervous. The sleepless night spent tossing and turning did not help either. I tried my level best to eat some fruits, which are said to be easy on the stomach, but was unable to. Usually the one to down a heavy breakfast comprising of cereal, milk and eggs, my inability to even bite an apple gave broad hints to my grandmother about my mental distress.

"Beta, don't take so much tension. You've prepared so hard, believe me, you'll do well!" grandma consoled me, not having any clue about the importance of this so-called "exam" I was going to take. She subtly tried to give me a handful of cashew-nuts and almonds to ensure I didn't leave on an empty stomach. I took them and left them on the dining table since nothing was going to go in till that ghost of a CAT was vanquished.

Grandmother took me to the portrait that hung in the storeroom, now a mini gurudwara of Sri Guru Gobind Singh ji, the tenth guru of our religion, and told me to offer a small prayer. I am not an atheist or anything, it's just that I remember God very scarcely, mostly at times like these, when there is no hope and no one else to turn to. It somehow gives me peace, and calms me down, and that's what happened in that one minute of closed eyes and prayer offering.

I felt recharged. My eyes, heavy from just four hours of sleep, felt much lighter. I was ready. There was nothing to lose, I thought. Why I thought so, though, I never knew, because there was almost everything to lose.

Three hours and a lot of intense problem-solving later, I came out, feeling nothing, not knowing how I had performed. With CAT, you usually don't. I avoided the murmurs as everyone started discussing questions and complaining with their hands on their heads, how they had missed that one question, which if they hadn't, they would be sitting in the Mecca of management education in India, IIM Ahmedabad. I called up a few friends to get an idea of how many questions they had attempted, and just to get a hang of how many were good enough.

To my surprise, I had done better than most of them, even those about whom I was sure would get into an IIM. I felt a little better after hearing all this, and after mulling over how to spend the rest of the day, which I surely did not want to do at home, sitting and watching saas bahu soaps with grandma, so I went to a friend's place to blow off some steam. I hadn't touched beer in all this while, and I compensated for that in the most grandiose manner possible.

❖ ❖ ❖

I had planned to leave for Pune a week after CAT, so that those suspecting my absence was ascribed to preparation for CAT, would not get a sure-shot proof of the same. Although, there were so many in Infotech suddenly falling victims of jaundice or typhoid just before CAT that I knew I was thinking extremely wishfully.

"Ah, there you are! So how was your CAT?" asked the project manager, with an intentional and complete disregard to the fact that I was supposed to be suffering from jaundice.

"Oh not too well sir, actually I was weak and drowsy from the medication for jaundice, so I guess another year here with Infotech," I said, shrugging my shoulders, an expression of resignation written all over my face.

I got my revenge by the look my reply had generated on his face.

Simi was the only person in the team who actually thought I had been ill. I couldn't blame her, she was not the smartest person around and combined with the fact that she had feelings for me, her thought- process was perfectly justifiable.

She had managed a welcome-back card for me and a cake for a cordial reception. She had also called everyone to my cubicle. That was officially the most embarrassing day of my life. 15 people standing, welcoming me back from the claws of a disease that never happened. I could see the wry smiles on everyone's faces, except of course, Simi's. I didn't know what feelings to gather for her, to be grateful, for being so caring, or to bear a grudge for being so dumb.

Anyhow, the nightmare lasted 15 odd minutes. People did not care much after they had stomached their portion of the black forest cake. Hell, few of them thought it was my birthday, and it was only after they saw the card did they realise what they had been called for.

❖ ❖ ❖

The days in office passed slowly in the never-ending wait for my results. Often sitting in my cubicle, I speculated about what fate had in store for me. Was I going to die as a software engineer or graduate from a premier B-school? Gory pictures of me still driving my Pulsar at the age of 45 with two kids stuffed in between me and my wife flashed before my eyes. I tried hard to see who the wife was, and if she was pretty, it would have been some consolation at least, but her face never came to light.

I became more indolent with my work and a little scared too, because, with recession creeping in, many employees were being given the pink slip. Why such a lethal piece of paper was given such a mushy name, was beyond my comprehension. Why wasn't it called the black slip? Someone would rather say he got kicked out of office because he was given the 'black slip' rather than a 'pink slip'. I think it's the company's parting kick on your ass.

❖ ❖ ❖

CHAPTER 3

The Dream Rekindles

"You see, madness, as you know, is like gravity.
All it takes is a little push!"
– The Joker : The Dark Knight

Time was passing at a snail's pace once more when an unprecedented mail from the HR department gave me a reason to rejoice. Infotech was planning on having a sports and cultural festival, a ritual planned for the end of every year, just to prove to its employees and the outer world that this company does not just suck the blood out of the employees, but also cares for the 'welfare' of its employees. Squeezing six sports and five cultural activities within a five-day window sure was very thoughtful, I thought, sarcastically.

Within seconds of the mail hitting the inbox, Hardik called me.

"What say, how about some cricket?"he asked.

"Hell,yeah!Cricket, basketball, badminton, anything to get away from my cubicle."

"Good, selection will be today evening. We'll leave early."

"Yeah, I like early," I smirked.

I learnt from the mail that permission had to be sought from the project manager to leave before the office timings to take part in these events. This made me a little queasy, after all, I already wasn't the most hardworking employee around.

"Sports? Haven't you just recovered from jaundice?" the project manager asked, exasperated by my antics.

My insides churned. What a retard I was, I thought, simultaneously cussing Hardik for his idea. Jaundice is something which beckons months of rest and no physical activity at all for days afterward.

"Erm…sir, I only plan to take part in cricket, and I am a batsman, so it won't include much running around. You know how it's a sport for lazy people...hehe," I ended up laughing at my own pathetic joke.

Both of us knew that I wasn't down with jaundice, so after the initial awkwardness, everything turned out to be fine, for now my shamelessness had crossed unprecedented levels. I left earlier than usual, attracting more eyeballs than a normal day, and consequently I cared even lesser than I did on a normal day.

Cricket had always been the sport I loved the most. I was in class five when I had blown the opposition, Mount St. Mary's bowling attack to smithereens. Since then, I had always been the apple of my cricket coach's eye. He would emphatically declare in front of everyone else, that if he had it his own way, he would have enrolled me with a local cricket academy at that age, but knowing my parentless background, deep down he knew that cricket was something that would always have to remain only a hobby for me.

It was in class ten that I was at the peak of my skill and a part of the school team, a team which was feared across other schools, and it was a fear which was generated in a large part, due to a lone boy named Vineet Grover. The school coach, by then, was almost sure that cricket was my calling and the immensity of talent that I exuded would soon take me to being a state-level cricketer.

But fate had other things in store for me and my gradual digression from studies was pretty evident in my score cards. The tipping point was when I failed in a pre-board examination in what was once my forte, Maths exam, which sent my grandmother into deep shock.

I tried to explain to her the frivolity of pre-board examinations and vowed to excel in the boards, but she heard the hollow ring in these promises and reminded me of the immense trouble she had undergone to bring me to where I was. Guilt galore, I never had the courage to look at my cricket bat again. That year, I shoved myself into the silent, sleepless realms of thick-bound texts and the labyrinthine alley ways of the help-books.

I was sure I would get back to cricket the moment I faced my boards, which to an extent I did, but I had failed to take into account that a decent score during the Board exams beckoned the science stream in class 11th rather vehemently. Consequently, the endless pursuit to be a part of a revered institute and to be an engineer ensued.

The pursuit included spending two years in a god forsaken place called Kota, preparing to step inside the hallowed portals of another institute, the first two letters of which are the same as that of the IIMs. Life in Kota ceased to exist, it was a place where hale and hearty young brains were sent to be mechanised. To add to that, the constant lingering fact that I was parentless and all the money I spent belonged to an old woman's hard-earned savings, who earned out every single penny under supreme adversity, made sure that cricket did not even feature as a lesser priority. The days at the engineering college were no different, since the same guilt about being a parasite on a 70-year old engulfed me and owing to this, I rarely led myself astray. Almost a non-entity for the majority of my college time, I spent any free time I had in earning extra pocket money. It mainly included giving tuitions to school students. One odd time I did let myself loose and gave into the desire of playing cricket, but I knew that the love for the game and the temptation that would follow would be too strong to let myself part with it yet again, hence I mostly refrained.

But now that I was finally earning, and earning enough to send a decent sum each month back to my old lady, apart from letting myself indulge in a lot of things I'd only wished I could have had access to earlier in life, I for once felt free enough to play the game again.

Back to the present-the selection was a breeze. Hell, one didn't even have to know how to play cricket to make it to the team. Such huge, overweight, over age stout heaps of flesh had turned up, I wondered whether they were trying out for the team or for being the ball. Unsurprisingly, both Hardik and I got selected for our respective business divisions.

My heart ached because I could not play any other sport since people recovering from jaundice usually don't jump right into heavy physical exertion, although jaundice did save me the embarrassment of participation in the dance competition with Sonali, whose super excitement I brought to ground level with a

"Baby, I can't, my project manager will know and then hell shall break loose. You know how exhausting dancing is and…."

The phone had been disconnected by then, though I didn't mind it at all. I'd do anything to not shake my booty in front of those IT nerds, which when added to the fact that my dancing skills were downright pathetic, strengthened my mental stand further.

After the selection, Hardik and I practiced until late in the evening, under the flood lights. After months altogether, I felt alive, playing my favourite sport. I was like a child who had found his lost GI Joe action figure. For once, those IT legs did not feel drained like they did after climbing a single flight of stairs. I felt I could bowl all night long and there was nothing that I wanted more. No amount of beer, chicken or even Sonali could have enticed me. I was back with my first love and it was simply blissful.

Gradually, the other players left the ground, but Hardik and I moved to the practice pitch with the nets. Infotech was good at maintaining sports infrastructure and equipment but ironically, never gave its employees enough time to even have a look at it. It was a part of the larger façade to make the employees feel how nurturing the company was.

"Let's call it a day! What say?" inquired Hardik, after I knocked back his off-stump for the third time in the last few deliveries.

"Okay," I puffed, since I was tired but immensely satisfied. The satisfaction of uprooting a stump can only be matched with watching your project manager get humiliated by his superior.

"You've got quicker, what are you eating these days, Revital?" he mocked at me, for getting the better of him.

"Stop whining, you've gotten old, you need some Revital more than me!" I laughed.

Although we really didn't need to, we still practiced the next two days after which the tournament began. To play with the Tendulkars of Infotech, we could have managed with one leg tied. Yes, they were that talented. What else would you expect when all you get to do the whole day is to sit in front of a computer screen, just getting up to fill yourself with calories that are only expended in the occasional fasting and bursts of laughter.

The tournament was of a knock out format and three consecutive victories got you the "coveted" Infotech cricket championship. While thinking about what a breeze it would be, I had overlooked one thing, that if the opposition was a bunch of supreme losers, so were the rest of the ten in my team, and I would have to put in a superhuman performance to drag this horde of no-hopers along.

The premonition of a disaster proved to be right as we conceded 95 runs to such a team whose selection criteria seems to have considered only those with a waistline above 40. They did not believe in running singles, it was a different story that they couldn't, even if they had wanted to. When the eight runs I conceded in my two overs were deducted, we had conceded a shameless 87 runs in the rest eight.

When my turn to bat came, I was reasonably confident in my ability to make the chase, despite the bowling debacle. I saved myself for a two-down position as I figured that we would require a sturdy batsman at that position. I was a good mix of decent technique and explosive instincts which, more often than not, enabled me to score at a rapid rate given that I did not lose my wicket to a brainless moment of idiocy.

I had just started to cool my heels in anticipation of a 20-odd minute break before I'd make an appearance, but alas, that was only a distant dream. Two down, and we were only in the second over.1.2 overs to be precise, with five runs on the board out of which four were byes. To my surprise, the bowler who was the fattest of that lot, a no mean achievement by any stretch of imagination, was also the fastest. He had a two-step run up and was bowling rockets.

His run up, like that of a rabbit, hop twice and then swoosh, was deceptive, to say the least. I was fidgety all through his over and somehow, by the grace of God, my wickets were still intact. It was only later that I came to know about his national-level cricketing exploits. He had, in his heyday, played for Tamil Nadu with a more flaunt-worthy waistline and a delivery speed that was even quicker than it was now. It was a shame what IT did to him. R.I.P Mr. Tamil Nadu, I paid my homage.

Playing like this wasn't taking us anywhere, I knew it. I had to get into my natural game, i.e. throw the kitchen sink with everything full. I'd have to defend or try to sneak out a single at everything on good length and well, if the ball was pitched short, like a kid on his first date who is asked to kiss, I didn't have a clue what to do.

I had underestimated the strength in my arms. I wasn't the 17 year old kid anymore; I was a twenty-three year old man who benched 200 pounds. And it showed when I flayed the mediocre bowling left, right and center. The plan worked fasulousix because the opposition knew how to bowl only two kinds of deliveries, high full tosses or low ones.

The latter went for sixes and the former ones for fours. Soon, we were sailing comfortably and were enroute to a fabulous victory charted by yours truly.

18 runs in 3 overs were required, and it had started to look like a cakewalk. Only, I had forgotten Mr. Tamil Nadu was still left with another over and it was at this moment that they played their trump card. He was as shrewd as he looked. He must have noticed my tendency to jump on to my front foot even before the ball was bowled and hence darted in a short delivery at a screaming pace, to which all I could've done was hang my bat limply in the air. The ball lobbed up, delivering the easiest of catches to which one of their fielders happily obliged. The next five deliveries from Mr. Tamil Nadu fetched two more wickets and in short, cost us the match.

❖ ❖ ❖

I never knew that the loss of a cricket match at Infotech Ltd. would hurt me so much. Shattered, I never realised that winning such an inconsequential tournament would become an obsession of mine. I silently conjured scenarios where I'd be in the centre of the pitch scoring runs, taking wickets, and people would be cheering for me. This adulation had always been a dream for me, a dream that had remained unfulfilled. A dream that involved me, like a gladiator, standing right in the middle of acoliseum, and chants of my name filling the arena with echoes flashed through my mind repeatedly, giving me recurrent goose bumps. Not that the Infotech tournament was anywhere close to what I'd dreamt of,it was just the fact that any degree of the dream being fulfilled would have made me ecstatic.

The Infotech trophy was one easy opportunity to live a part of my dream, but I had failed. The void had grown wider and emptier and the uneasiness increased. The tournament was clinched by Hardik's team and he was declared the man of the series. I was happy for him, but the embers of pain that burned inside me were only aggravated further because I knew I was a better player than him.

Uncomfortable nights and irritable day dreaming followed and the issue which had caused this anxiety, I thought, was so petty that the mere mention of it to anyone would sound insane. From where had so much passion for cricket crept within me, I couldn't figure. It was something I had repressed so perfectly for over six years, and yet, there it was, exposing the nakedness of my feelings in a single day. It was a sudden rush I had experienced, and consequently, all I did after office hours was to play cricket. Sometimes with Hardik and sometimes when alone, I'd bowl till my sweat weighed more than me. In my own zone, I never realised I was spending an insane amount of time practicing. The defeat was driving me crazy, and I kept visualising that same delivery over and over again, wishing how I could have met it with so many strokes other than the hapless one I actually did.

I thought I'd talk toSonali about this, but gave up the idea because I presumed she'd laugh at my paranoia.

❖ ❖ ❖

"What happened yaar? You're not yourself these days! Have I done something? You don't call, you don't message!" Sonali confronted me when I avoided her for lunch one day.

"Nothing, I'm fine," I said, faking a weak smile.

"Who are you kidding, Vineet? Please tell me what's bothering you. I may be of some help," she spoke, with genuine concern.

"It has nothing to do with you. It's just that some things are not okay at home," I lied on impulse, not wanting to reveal my idiosyncrasies to her.

"What?! And you didn't bother to tell me?! What happened, Vineet?" she asked, now beginning to sound worried as hell.

I felt a stab of guilt as I lied further.

"Nothing. I really do not want to talk about it now. Can we talk after office? We'll go to CCD," I said, and she nodded in agreement.

We met over coffee and I opened up my heart to her. I had reservations about telling her, wondering if she would understand me or not. I guess that's what love is, when the other person construes your emotions without you, giving any words to them. She did not speak much but I knew she could connect with me somehow, perhaps I could feel her eyes conversing with me. I felt lighter as she quietly listened to all I had to say. It's also true that half the problem can be solved by someone listening to you. I did feel better after the conversation with Sonali, but the other half though, was still embedded deep down inside my heart.

"Oh my Gooood!" Simi was breathless after running from her cubicle to mine.

"What are you doing?! It's an office Simi, speak softly!" I spoke in a muted voice, my jaw clenchedin disapproval.

"I don't care. You got a 99 percentile, man!!" she shrieked, her eyes unimaginably wide and her enthusiasm palpable.

"How would you know? Do you have my ID number?" I asked, feigning non chalance, although I had already missed a couple of heartbeats.

"Stop asking questions and give me a hug, Vineet!" she said, as she hugged me tightly. Infact, tightly enough for me to know that she was magnanimously endowed.

Still struggling to digest the news, I jumped back on to my seat to verify this claim made by Simi.

"If it's not what you say, Simi, I'll kill you for sure. This should not be a joke!" I looked back at her with arched brows while I waited for the results site to open. She stood there smiling, and boy! She was looking cuter than ever before. How did messengers of good news suddenly look like angels? I wondered.

I very slowly entered my ID and date of birth, eliminating any chances of a mistake or a consequent cardiac arrest. My heart was now pounding fiercely. I don't know about Simi, but I could hear it beating with utmost clarity.

I had scored 99.1 percentile. Holy mother of God!, I thought. Had I been alone, the howl of my euphoria would have been heard as far and wide as Gabbar's laugh echoed. Here, I just mentally shouted and fist- pumped. I had accomplished what I had worked so hard for. For a brief moment, a multitude of pictures flashed in front of my eyes depicting several pivotal points in my life. Everything had fallen into place, I now realised.

What followed the declaration of the results was another hug to Simi, without any intent of feeling her endowments though, and a promise of an extravagant dinner which included an 'on the house' supply of top-notch wine.

This red-hot news travelled at a blistering rate till another friend who had got a 99.6 percentile called. It wasn't his percentile that put the world on hold for a second, it was his question.

"So what all calls did you manage?"

"Calls? Aren't they declared after a day or two?" I crossed the fingers of my left hand along with every mental finger I could manage!

"Nah, man! They are there right at the bottom of the score card, I managed all 6," that bastard laughed.

"Wait then I'll check again! Thanks for the heads up," I spoke hesitantly and kept the phone as my heart picked up pace for the second time in the day.

I had already started feeling a little dizzy, and my stomach churned. Had I missed seeing the calls?Or was it that with a 99.1percentile, I still hadn't got a single IIM call?

I had never imagined that entering my ID and date of birth again would be ten times more difficult than it was the first time. I pressed enter while chanting God's name at a rapid rate.

The Earth stopped rotating; my heart stopped pumping and I momentarily blacked out! Was it a joke, I wondered, sitting motionless, in a state of shock. After entering my credentials and rechecking the result a few more times, more out of disgust and frustration than the belief of an error, it all sunk in. Just like the coarsest of rums, whose names haven't even been heard of, which manage their way into your abdomen at their own pace, this news also took time to be absorbed. 99.1 percentile with a 94 percentile plus in each section, and still no IIM call. There wasn't a higher marking on the bad luck barometer, and I still crossed it. I had officially become an atheist.

It was 4 in the evening, and paying no regard to this fact,I picked up my belongings and headed straight to a bar. I sat there unaccompanied, drinking and ruminating over what had struck me. I had shoved the cell phone into my bag to avoid any more calls, the calls which reminded me what a loser I was. Such things take some time to sink in completely, and in my case, it had to be facilitated by ethanol, preferably in a form with more than 4.75% concentration. In other words, in times of despair,beer does not help. It definitely is well said -beer sure is only the king of good times!

It was ten at night and time to leave the bar since I had made my peace with the fact that I would not be a part of the venerated IIMs anymore. MDI or NITIE would do -good enough colleges, I thought.

During this drinking marathon, I had received twenty-one missed calls from random people, people who manage to look up your phone number on the day when the CAT results are out. This is mostly to rub in their IIM calls on your face or, if they themselves have been screwed, probably to find solace in others who shared similar fates with them, and to bitch about how unfair CAT is. To avoid these uncomfortable encounters, I decided not to call back anyone.

I did call up Sonali though, who herself had not done very well in her CAT, but she was fine with her life at Infotech. She was expecting an onsite call any day now. "Hey! So what? MDI, etc. are damn good colleges, too," she had said, trying to console me, and I pretended to be easily consolable to avoid any further conversation on the subject of my percentile and the grim future that awaited me.

Within some time, when I felt the current measure of alcohol in my body would not be enough to mollify this pain, I called up Hardik.

"Oye! Go get rum ASAP. I'll be there in half an hour!" I said, hurriedly climbing on to my bike.

"Make sure, the rum should be enough to last till tomorrow morning," I said, wanting to certify that this time the alcohol had no chance of betraying me.

"It will last you this whole weekend brother! Come quickly!" he chuckled.

The best part about friends is that when you're sad, they'll end up drinking more than you. The whole night we steadily downed glass after glass. There was so much rum, we could have had a party for 10 people. If only someone would have come up and told me, "Oh, that was the wrong result, you've got four IIM calls!" But of course, that didn't happen.

❖ ❖ ❖

I was sweating profusely under the helmet, my eyes bloodshot and my body quivering with fear. Two runs were required of the last ball and the world's quickest bowler was bowling. It was the question of championship and glory v/s heartbreak and dismay for the whole nation.

A slower ball, oh, I'd picked it out, I thought. He always transfers the ball from the left hand to the right one when he does that. I'll smash it out of the park, I thought, and my heartbeat surged. The penultimate stride, the smoothest of jumps and the perfect landing let out what was a searing 95 miles per hour delivery that crashed into the base of my leg stump. The bat was stationed in Jammu when the ball had already kissed Kanyakumari as I turned to see the disarray my stumps were in. My head hung in what would be perennial shame and a permanent end to my career.

"What, are you having sex in your dreams? You're moaning so much!" laughed Hardik.

Still breathing heavily, I woke up from the nightmare. I'd saved myself the from embarrassment and heartache of a lifetime; I heaved a sigh of relief. My head hurt from the infinite amount of rum I'd consumed the night before and the morning after, and, well, that afternoon too. I had skipped all my meals feasting only on rum, Pepsi and chips. I felt like crap and I hadn't taken one in a day, either.

Anyhow, I had to get myself back on track once again -life had to go on. A lot of research revealed that certain colleges were at par with some of the IIMs. At least that's what I had to believe to start preparing for the interviews for those colleges, which were all lined up within a month's time.

It wasn't long before I was immersed in the world of the India Today, Outlook and the occasional Economist. Reading and trying to comprehend text in these complex compilations of excerpts loaded with financial and economic jargon was way beyond me. I still recall the countless nights I had spent perfecting jabber on the Sub prime crisis, which at that point was a hot topic.

On gathering more knowledge about what such B-school interviews were comprised of, the information was too strange to be assimilated. It's almost like, if you play cricket, you should know triviel like what Sachin Tendulkar's brother's daughter's name was, and subsequently, what profession she was into. I just play cricket, I am not Sachin Tendulkar's family servant, for God's sake! I'd think.

The most dreaded question of all was the "Why MBA?" This two-word question, if answered in a manner not conforming to the interviewer's views, had the capability of summing up your future in two words as well, that is to say, "You're screwed."

The answer, I felt, should have been simple enough. In the two years of having a gala time, my market value would be five-fold, and that I, like Uncle Scrooge, had a fetish for diving into a room full of currency. Contrary to the truth, the panel there wants to listen to how you have wanted to be a manager since the day you were born.

"Being an IAS officer, actor, defense personnel and a sportsperson can all go to hell. Before saying 'ma' I inserted a B in between and said 'mBa', that is how passionate I am about an MBA, sir. Sitting in a chair from 9 to 9 gives me an adrenaline pump and I am crazy about long office hours. My favourite hobby is ass-kissing and when not doing that, I am devising new ways do to that subtly." This was what I believed was the perfect answer for this enigma of a question.

In a perfect world, questions like Why do you want to join our institute?, should be succinctly answered by a "It was my only bloody call, you moron," or if you were lucky enough to have multiple calls, it should be more like, "Oh sir, your placement records kick ass, average shown is 14 lacs p.a, I think I am tad above average so I think I'd manage a 16 lacs p.a, which is precisely what I want."

Of course, that is not what happens in actuality. Answers are more on the lines of the exceptional erudition imparted by the academia, the rich alumni base, the time-proven capability of the institution to produce world leaders and that the lineage of that college was incomparable. No mention of the actual reason can even be subtly cited; else the game would be over before it even began.

Learning such tricks of the trade along with learning the answers to the simplest of questions like 'Tell me something about yourself' by rote, was how the next few days passed.

❖ ❖ ❖

It was almost 7 o'clock when a friend called, who fell under the once-in-a-blue-moon category.

"Dude, you've got an FMS call," he proclaimed.

"Yeah and you are the President of India," I said as I tried to sound indifferent, but by that time I had already started feeling a small bead of sweat on my neck which had trickled down from somewhere around the back of my ear. Too good to be true, I thought. It was too good because of the super measly number of calls FMS usually dished out.

Ten minutes of intense promises about not lying, by Hemant, was what it took to finally convince me that I had indeed cracked the FMS paper. Was this my calling?, I thought

My atheism started withering away. I looked up to the skies and smiled. God indeed is funny. How he must have calculated that owing to my versatility, multi dimensional personality and bank (im)balance(FMS has a very low fee), FMS was indeed the best bet for me and not IIM A, for the fear that I might turn into a nerd.

❖ ❖ ❖

Every time I felt that a particular day was the most important day in my life, a new one came up and beat the previous one to pulp, and the same happened when the FMS interview day arrived. The days of the CAT, the results, etc., seemed trivial when juxtaposed against that day.

From head to toe, not one piece of fabric on my body had been previously used. A white Arrow pinstriped shirt, a black striped business suit, again of Arrow make, a shiny black pair of leather Lee Cooper shoes, my father's Tag Heuer (this was old, but it was a TAG), a Van Heusen gray and navy blue single-knotted tie and brand new Jockey underwear, all of which had easily taken my one month's salary.

If the mirror could possibly speak, it would have spoken, on that particular day. I was looking like a CEO of a newly founded firm. Anyone who would've shot a glance at me would have been positive that I would whip out my Blackberry anytime, call my chauffeur to drive down my Honda Accord, possibly because I was getting late for my flight to Singapore for a client meet.

Dressed to kill (or possibly to get killed), I smiled at the mirror again and with a final nod of appreciation, left for the interview centre. The selection procedure for the second round of a B-school usually comprises a group discussion and an interview, but at FMS, there was an extra filter in the way of an extempore.

My GD group comprised of 8 people who looked as suave as me(if not more), in their newly purchased/tailored suits. Little did I know that this façade of sophistication had bidden its time and this seemingly couth congregation of men and women would soon transform into tribes of ninja assassins, throwing daggers, knives and swords at each other. The topic, from what I recall,was something related to the World Trade Organisation- whether it was actually an effective organisation or a dummy one.

Know one thing about people in group discussions -in a B-school GD, come what may, the GDP of India and the contribution of each sector i.e. agriculture, manufacturing and services would be thrown in by someone. Even if the topic is 'my red dress,' someone for sure is going to quote the contribution of the manufacturing sector to the GDP and then claim that since a red dress is a component of this industry, the GD group should first enlighten the panel on this sector. After all, managers talk about the state of the economy rather than pieces of apparel.

As our GD began, not less than five out of the eight candidates, myself included, started jabbering on the topic. Gifted with a heavy voice, I emerged as the clear winner in this petty melee whilst the others gave in. I made a very brief start, making sure that what I knew was taken in by the panelists, because, let me be clear, I did not know much about this World Trade Organisation.

Two minutes later I could sense that not only I, none of the rest actually had any valuable content on the topic. The GD members were throwing jargon in the air, hoping for it to make sense all by itself, but that only happens when the panelists are as dumb as the students, which in this case was not even remotely true.

Group Discussions, more often than not, tend to become fish markets, and for the first couple of minutes, this discussion was not an exception either, but merely five minutes into the discussion, it transformed into what appeared more like a death ceremony. People who were jumping during the first minute suddenly changed into the ones with the best mannerisms.

"I think you had a point to make"… "It's ok, you continue…" "I think my friend here made a very valid point. Taking the point forward…,"was the general environment of the GD.

I, along with another guy, was making some semblance of sense though, and had implicitly been awarded the leadership by the rest of the group, since only after we'd speak could they pick out the remnants from it, rephrase it in flowery English, and throw it again at the group. What future managers I tell you!

Finally, after eight painful minutes of us beating around the bush, the panel had to stop us. Probably, they must have felt more ashamed and uncomfortable than us, seeing the 'quality' of the new prospective students of their institute. An old gentleman amongst the panel gave us a piece of his mind caustically, stating how even his daughter who happened to be in class 9 could talk more fluently on the norms and rules of the WTO than us.

A little ashamed, but mostly overjoyed, on being the best amongst the worst, I mentally geared up for the extempore which would then be succeeded by the interview. I had prepared extensively for the extempore. Every topic on mother earth even vaguely related to me had been practiced on, mostly in front of a mirror and in the shower.

Starting from my name 'Vineet' to my mother's, father's, college's name, InfoTech Ltd., to every possible word in a linked list that could be tracked back to me, I had prepared a small one-minute talk.

I was fifth in turn for the extempore-cum-interview, and I tried asking everyone who preceded me about their extempore topic and interview questions in general, and then tried to mentally answer each of them. Finally, my turn came, and my stomach churned like it was placed in a blender. Poor analogy, I agree, but visually perfect imagery to describe my abdominal state. I should have spent some more time in the washroom, I thought. Never mind, I told myself, I'll take it through.

I anxiously asked for permission before I entered the carpeted room where a panel of five was waiting to tear into me like a pack of piranhas. I exchanged greetings with the loveliest of smiles, trying to ease the tension in the room, which was pretty palpable. The panel consisted of the Dean and four other members. Why five people, who have fifty times more knowledge than you, were required to interview one, I wondered. The odds were stacked against me at 1:250.I quickly computed this and it immediately painted a grim picture in my mind of what laid ahead.

I had just sat down and was readying myself for the tete-a-tete that was about to follow, when I heard someone say 'Banana!'"What in the world?" I gasped. I looked up and requested the panel to repeat the word that rhymed with banana.

"Son, speak for a minute about abanana," he said again.

Banana?what do I have to do with a banana? I thought, perplexed. Do I look like one?Or does it look like I have one stuck up my ass? I wondered.

Anyway, extempores were known to shake the ground beneath your feet and this one sure made me stumble.

After a two-second pause, I started blabbering on everything I knew about a banana, where it grows, what it looked like. I touched upon banana swings and I was switching on to banana boats when the Dean stopped me.

I was moderately happy with my performance and the panelists looked pleased too but that look was wiped off their face when they saw the graduation marks on my resume.

"61%!! With those kind of marks, you dream of being a part of FMS?" asked a lady panelist, albeit very politely. Never give excuses for your failures, I had been taught repeatedly. But the devil inside me prodded. Being candid wasn't getting me anywhere and I knew that.

"Ma'am, I am from Pune University, and the topper of my class had a 67%, hence my performance is not as bad as it seems," I replied with the most radiant smile pasted on my face.

She seemed convinced, although the other two didn't, and the remaining two didn't look like they gave two hoots about it. Interview was a quickie, I answered all I could, floundering now and then, and before I knew it, it was over. The question now was, who would the screw'ed'be, and who the screw'ee'. Results would answer that soon.

I couldn't say I was elated, nor would the word dejected have done justice to my feelings at that time. To garner a perspective, positive or negative, towards my interview, I decided to conduct an in-depth analysis of the whole episode. To put myself away from this feeling of uncertainty and get to feel either euphoria or angst, I went straight to a nearby Café Coffee Day and began mulling over the possibly life-changing events that had unfolded in the past few hours.

After an hour-long intense analysis, I landed up where I'd begun i.e., nowhere. I finally decided to give it a rest and go to do what I did when I was in a fix-have some beer. I went to meet a friend in Gurgaon, more of an acquaintance rather, but rich enough to pay for me in an expensive restaurant, so I didn't mind the company.

It was a quiet affair, both because he was too boring and because the analysis that I had put to rest an hour back kept begging to be scrutinized minutely. Not able to bear the mental tussle anymore, I abruptly got up, thanked him, told him I had something really important to take care of, and left.

Without much ado, fighting the flurry of thoughts clamoring for attention in my mind, I slept because I had to catch a flight to Pune the next morning,

As the morning arrived, at the airport, I grabbed a super-expensive muffin and the costliest coffee of my life when I learnt that the flight was late. While boarding, just like always, I was praying for one of the few hot females I had been subtly observing at the airport to be seated next to me. And just like always, an old man with the biggest of tummies came and sat next to me. I was hopeless with prayers and aircraft seats, I thought dejectedly.

It was while I was passing his juice and breakfast tray to him that we struck up a conversation.

"So, what do you do, young man?" he asked, with his dark black eyes transfixed onto mine, more demanding an answer that politely inquiring.

"Sir, I work with Infotech Ltd. in Pune," I said, a little befuddled at this sudden interrogation. I quickly added that "I had come to Delhi to give my B-school interviews," unnecessarily, for reasons unknown.

On inquiring about him I came to know that he was an IT project manager based in the United States of America. He used to work for eight months as a freelancing project manager in any random IT firm which could basically afford someone as experienced as him and then for the rest of the year, he'd take a holiday and would live life. Living life for him included coming to India to meet his parents and then travelling around the world to pursue his passion, i.e., photography.

After half an hour of conversing with him, I came to know that he was a big shot in the world of photography, having won a few international awards here and there. Amazed at his lifestyle, I sat there awe struck, listening to his countless stories of travel around the world.

"Just remember; never give up on your passion. Life is a trade-off; you have to make a decision at some point in life to decide what it is you want. I could have stayed full-time into IT and could have probably been a CEO of a firm today, but I gave that up for my passion and now I'm living a dream,"the smile on his face was indeed worth more than a zillion words, proving undeniably how happy he was.

These words were to stay with me for a long, long time.

We talked some more, about his work and life in general. He revealed a few of his romantic escapades and why he hadn't tied the knot till date. He was approaching 50 and lamented this one decision of not marrying the love of his life.

"With age you get lonely. Friends are married and, well, the rest don't give a damn about you, it's then you wish you had this special someone." I could see the pain right through his smile, it did not reach his eyes.

For once, I was happy that this old man was seated next to me, imparting lessons of a lifetime to me.

"So, what is it that you really love, eh?" he asked.

"I would love to be a Marketing manager, Sir," I replied.

"Oh no no… not a career, what is it you'd give anything in your life to be, that kind of a thing!" he goaded me to derive a more honest answer.

I thought for hardly a moment when I heard myself saying,"Playing cricket for India, Sir. The navy blue cap, white overalls and scoring a double century at Perth," I laughed making it sound casual so that he didn't cackle at the bizarre nature of my reply.

"That's good. Ever considered taking up cricket as a career?" he asked, and to my disbelief, he sounded serious.

"Oh no,Sir. It's a dream, not an ambition, I mean you asked in particular, otherwise I'd like to work for a nice marketing firm for a few years and then start my own business venture," I quickly resorted to the more conventional answer.

What was I blabbering?! I thought, as I mentally kicked myself.

I think he understood that I was more conscious now, out of that hypnotised state, and wouldn't like to discuss my inner desires anymore.

"It never hurts to give it a try," he winked at me as we ended our conversation on silent agreement.

We did not speak again as I looked out of the window, and all I could see were clouds, much below where I was. Maybe a symbolic representation of what the man wanted to say: anything is possible. I thought over what he had said. The rational me reasoned against my illusionary beliefs as every young boy in India has aspired to be a cricketer someday, what was I even thinking, that too being a twenty-three year old man who had already started his professional career. I shunned the train of thought and diverted my mind again towards analysing my interview. I had re-calculated my odds again and again and the picture looked bleaker by the hour.

We landed within the stipulated two hours. The Pune airport, though significantly smaller than its Delhi counterpart, had its own charm as it somehow felt cozier than Delhi. Maybe because Pune felt like home now.

Some things never change and, like always, my luggage, which was a single bag in this case, was the last one to appear on the super-sluggish conveyer belt.

Hardik was already there to pick me up with a can of chilled beer in his bag. Since I didn't have much luggage, we went straight to Toons as I chugged the contents of the can en route. Toons was a different story in the afternoons. No rock songs blared from the speakers, only a muted TV played. Not many people were around and surely no eye candy. But when one gets cheap and chilled beer and a silent ambience to have a nice one-to-one, one really can't ask for more.

I told Hardik all about my interview and like a nervous girl who has just slept with someone for the first time in her life, kept asking him what he felt would happen.

"What the hell would I know? Stop acting like a girl!" he got me back into my senses as we chatted over a few more beers.

In the evening, I met Sonali and we went to this nice cozy place called Bashos. The place is a real delight for couples. The ambience is what makes it so special. Adorned with cushiony mattresses on the floor in place of chairs, and small cubicle-like structures, which lets each group or couple have their own small space so that one can really cuddle up, this was a place we frequently haunted. To facilitate this ambience of coziness, the place is dimly lit with the only source of lighting being the candles placed inside long glass enclosures on the tables.

Of course, you do get shameless people once in a while, who don't think twice before using their hands in unmentionable ways, but that apart, it is indeed a wonderful place to spend some quality time.

"Vineet, let's not kid ourselves.In two odd months, you will have left this place and in all probability I'll be here in Pune. Have you thought about us?" she came up with this all of a sudden right in between all the mush and snuggling up.

I was speechless, literally. I actually hadn't thought about it, though there was not an iota of a doubt that I loved her. All I managed to do was to look her in the eyes and say, "I don't know."

Yes, that was my dumb reply.

"You don't know?? Are you serious? We've been seeing each other for like a year now and you don't know! You knew how to use a condom, you bloody as shole!" she burst out.

God! I had blown the lid of this pressure cooker. I had never seen her in such a rage. I feared the beer bottle just might be smashed on my head any moment.

"Sonali yaar, I didn't mean that. I love you, we'll work something out. I swear. Don't spoil the evening please?" I pleaded.

Well, that boat had already sailed, and she didn't say another word during dinner, nor did she eat anything. I tried to act smart and offered her a morsel of roti with gravy but she flipped it so viciously that it flew two sections across, in the middle of a wild gang partying. Luckily, they were all so sloshed that had she even thrown the whole dish at them, I wonder if they would have noticed. I didn't try anything else during the evening.

I dropped her home, really wanting to ask her whether I could come up to her place, but then I imagined my testicles would be flying the same way that piece of tandoori roti had, and I changed my mind.

To be fair, I did actually have some serious thinking to do about us, our future and other related issues. Long distance was something she did not handle well. Also, she would ask me to come visit her every month. Ten thousand per month only on air tickets, I shuddered only thinking of it, I was indeed in a fix.

An hour of wooing her over the phone was what it took to meet her the following day in our favourite haunt, Café Coffee Day. We sat in our favourite corner, as all couples probably do in coffee shops, where innumerable memories, sweet and sour ones are rooted, giving you a lot of old stuff to gabble about. She looked prettier than ever and when she was sad, she could look irresistibly adorable. I felt like planting a kiss on her cheeks and after restraining myself for a few seconds, I gave into my desire. I could see the "Ooh cheap bastard!" glances piercing me from all around the coffee shop but I couldn't care less.

Usually averse to public display of affection, I thought Sonali would be horror-struck by my oh-so-uncouth mannerisms, but to my astonishment and relief, she smiled back. After two hours and a lot of coffee, we decided that it was best to let things take their own natural course. It was very early for both of us to actually decide our future, plus nothing was in our hands at the moment anyway. I promised to be there for her always and she promised to try to make the long-distance thing work. Feeling a bit better about myself, we began planning for a vacation before I left for good. We had just noted down the list of possible getaways, when Hardik called.

"How much money do you have in your account dude? It is wegent." He sounded really tense.

"What happened dude…everything all right?"

"Yaar please hurry up…tell me how much you have, it's very urgent!" he sort of shouted.

"Ok, ok... I have around twenty-five grand left and if you want I can arrange for more..." I answered.

"Well then, get ready! Buddy, we are going to Taj, you got through FMS, you bastard!!" he was almost shouting as the statement culminated.

"Damnnnnn!" I shouted, with the CCD staff almost ready for a 20-yard dash towards me to throw me out.

"Be there in a minute," I said.

I kissed Sonali and this time there was tongue involved, which made sure that the manager actually made a 10mtr.sprint towards me to remind me that this was a public place.

"Ya ya sorry, how much?" I said while holding Sonali in my arms by now. She had understood in the very first moment and happiness manifested itself in her beaming smile.

Whatever the bill amount was, I paid to the nearest hundred and left. Just like the worst days of your life, the best days also have this uncanny knack of topping the last one. In this case, the FMS convert topping the day on which I had been awarded the call, the call which I had converted and hence presenting me with undoubtedly the happiest day of my life.

I made phone calls to all and sundry, suddenly becoming that once-in-a-blue-moon irritating caller.

So many of the calls were on the lines of "Vineet who?"to which I'd merely answer "Whatever, loser! I'm through FMS, so now I guess you can find out 'Vineet who' ."

Ok, that was an exaggeration, but I guess you get the drift as to how many people I called that day.

Every awesome/not so awesome/sad/morbid occasion calls for alcohol. That is the beauty of this spirit, it gets you into this sloppy state where you just let go. Let go of your feelings, actions, and sometimes your morals and may be your clothes, too. Different story altogether. This was a celebration and since I had called every possible friend in town and my bank balance was nothing to flaunt about, the party had to be at home.

Around fifteen people had turned up ready to be stuffed with beer, whiskey, rum and cheese burst pizzas. Anticipating the amount of semi-processed cheese bursts-induced puke my house would be subject to that night, I had instructed people in prior that when feeling giddy, either run straight to the balcony and puke on the road or make a dash to my toilet. The latter being the safer option though, I had made it clear that my living and drawing room were not options, and this rule if tested would lead to their ass being kicked straight out of my house.

I had also asked my neighbours in advance, that if the decibel levels cross their patience levels, they can excuse me this one time, as pretty soon I'd be leaving to be a part of one of the most prestigious B- schools of India. This piece of information was met with arched eyebrows, oblivion, and at some places indifference. I had very smartly bribed them for excusing the noise. Mr.Ghutmales' children had been presented with Cadbury chocolates and Mr.Kadam's wife a fake compliment and a kaju barfi hamper. Mr.Bhansode, the asshole of the lot, was out somewhere for the week and that saved me a lot of tension.

The party was a wild one, and my friends were shamelessly hitting on my girlfriend;what effects of alcohol, I tell you. I redirected them to other females in the party and tried to be the perfect host by offering them chips, peanuts and the occasional slap on the back of the head for dirtying my house. It did not take long for the first of many vomits to happen. Three hours had passed and my restroom had now become a public toilet. Guys had peed everywhere except where it was meant to, and I didn't even want to wonder where the girls were peeing. Those who had come claiming that they'd have to leave early had now madc it a point that they could not even be shifted to a different corner let alone a different house. No one was planning on leaving soon; and I established that from the "What a party,man... so much booze...haha this will take some time to finish…but what are friends for" comments I received from everybody.

I had planned on finishing the party by midnight and then spending the night with Sonali.That was a distant dream now. She understood that this wasn't possible as she kissed me goodnight and left. I thought I'd seek Hardik's help to get this mess cleared with.

"Oi… help me get these assholes out now… else they'll all sleep here and there today," I said.

"Go from here…I don't care who's sleeping where but this chick is sleeping with me today, so go away, let me continue," he frowned, as he spoke in a muffled voice while he chatted with a girl, wasted enough not to understand a word even if he had shouted all of this.

Slowly, though tipsy beyond limits, I encouraged the less drunk ones to take along a passed-outone home with them as I claimed I did not have any mattresses for them to spend the night on. No one seemed to bother after so much booze even if I'd thrown them on the road, they wouldn't have cared.

'Each one takes one' was the slogan of the night. Finally eight people slept at my place, a garbage dump by then, and littered all over except at places where a human body lay. Hardik did not manage to bed the girl as her boyfriend came to pick her up, which left him very sad, and I had a nice time reminding him what a fool he had been the whole time.

Feeling delighted about what a manager I'd make at FMS since not one person had vomited inside the house after my instructions; I saw the most disgusting scene when I entered the kitchen. Who on earth had vomited in the kitchen?! I wanted to find out and rub his face in it. Anyhow, I spread newspapers over that crap and slept.

At around seven, people began getting up and started doddering their way back home leaving me in this mess, for which I knew I'd have hell to pay to my maid. She took 200 Rupees only for cleaning for this one day, apart from the 700 I gave her for a month. I must confess those 200 Rupees were well worth it and I am sure she must have made another 50 from the uncountable beer bottles and cans she collected from the place. The rest of the day was spent in nursing the hangover, with limejuice, orange juice and other fluids. Finally, I ate at night, when I was sure that my stomach was ready to ingest solid food.

❖ ❖ ❖

The approaching Monday was indeed the best one ever. I was free, at least for the next two years. I had a smile on my face that could give serious competition to the one on the Joker's face in the Batman series. Simi straight-away knew that it was some news related to my B-school quest and enquired about it. I told her what had happened and she was genuinely very happy for me. It feels good to have such people around, who care for you in such a true manner. At that time, I wished it was someone better she had liked, someone who deserved this gem of a girl, a little dumb, but great otherwise.

Anyhow, I had got a packet of sweets, expensive ones for the douche bags in office, in a futile endeavour to spread the happiness which was way too much to be contained in a single human body.

The grand prize for me was the look on their faces, and the cherry on the cake was indeed the look on the project manager's face, when the news that I was now to join FMS, spread. Oh, a moment to cherish and freeze in time, it could have given me happiness anytime no matter how glum I was.

That very day I filed my separation from the monolithic IT giant. It was a 30-day notice before I could leave but both I and my manager knew that now no one on earth could make me do any productive work for that firm.

So, after lunch that day, to relieve both the company and myself the agony of this period, I went to my manager's cubicle to explain to him, as to why I wanted to leave earlier than the stipulated notice period. Before I could start off with my rotten string of lame excuses which neither of us would have believed, he agreed to a one-week notice period.

Oh!How my walk felt that day, like a drunkard who has no fear of falling, paradoxical, but that is the only thing that could explain it.

CHAPTER 4

The Inception

"Happy are those who dream dreams and are ready to pay the price to make them come true."

– Leon Joseph Cardinal Suenens

The months that followed my resignation form, Infotech were pure bliss, courtesy, a good three months of 'ghar ka khana,'enhanced further by the fact that my grandmother was one of the best cooks I had ever come across. The simplest of dishes were so exotically prepared, with the right measures of spices and condiments, a proficiency honed by more than five decades of flawless cooking. With ghee and butter in unmeasured quantities, it was a piece of heaven.

Intense boredom in the second month forced me to look for interesting things to do on the internet. Learning foreign languages, salsa, guitar classes, reading books, writing a blog were few of the things that were recommended to me by friends.

After a lot of research, I zeroed in on learning French since, as far as I had heard, it was a good prerequisite to have, for getting a foreign placement at a B-school. That, apart from the fact that speaking French made women swoon over you. Learning the guitar had some of the same advantages sans the foreign placement part, but when taking into account the fact that I was always musically challenged, it failed to stand in good stead as an option.

Finally, after having decided upon learning French as my official pastime, I decided to enroll myself with one such language school. I rode towards the French School on my new Bullet, a purchase I could make, thanks to the provident fund money that had been accumulating in my account, courtesy the sham I had subjected Infotech Ltd. to. On the way, I happened to pass by a huge lush green ground which resembled a cricket ground minus the stands and the floodlights.

A sudden impulse enveloped me and I realised I was taking a U-turn, driving on the wrong side of the lane and entering the confines of the massive gate. The top of the entrance supported an arch-shaped board which read 'Mohan Meakins Cricket Club'in a worn-out shade of black, from which layers of chipped paint hung loosely; ready to drop any moment. As was the entire board itself, almost waiting to give way during even a strong gush of a Delhi thunderstorm.

As I parked my bike on one corner, an old man exemplifying the adage "one foot in the grave" confronted me. He was the guard, as his attire suggested, a timeworn man in his late sixties, it seemed, who could ward off, let alone a crook or a thief, not even a small puppy. In a season that would fall definitely under the type 'summer,' he somehow managed to sport a flimsy sweater.

"Can't you read 'No Parking'?" he grumbled. I could see all the way to the back of his throat through the massive cavities in his mouth courtesy the last few teeth left dangling from his gums, which seemed as fragile as the board at the gate.

I looked around and I saw a parking sign, hanging upside-down lifelessly, on a single hinge, and I had parked my bike in that area, as it turned out. The peace and quiet of the ground felt really comforting especially as a contrast to the hurrying traffic I was a part of, just moments back.

A two-room excuse for an office blocked the parking lot from the main ground. I entered the ground, crossing the corridor which stank like it hadn't had the opportunity of being cleaned for months now. The lush green ground wasn't as lush green now as I observed a group of young boys practicing in the nets. A man considerably older than the lot seemed to be shouting after every small period of play, with a lot of suggestions mixed generously with profanities.

After I had observed him for a good fifteen minutes from a safe distance, enough to get a good hang of all the abuses the old man stocked in his repertoire, he, who I figured was the coach, saw me.

"Hey you! What are you looking at?! Why are you late?" he asked, shouting at the top of his voice.

Taken aback, I was at a complete loss for what to do. I walked towards him to help him clarify any misgivings he might have fostered and he squinted hard at me as I got closer, to identify any familiar features on my face.

"Oh! My damned eyes! I am sorry," he said, once I was close enough, since he seemed to suffer from some long distance face recognition issues.

"But anyway, who the hell are you?" he asked.

"Nothing, Sir! I mean no one! I was just watching," I said.

"You don't play??" he asked.

"I do, sir," I found myself saying.

"Oye Rakesh, you buffoon! Give him the pads and the helmet, you idiot, let's see if he has the balls, you seem to have left back home today" he said, as he looked frustrated by something Rakesh had done.

There are times when you just can't say no and then there are times when you don't want to. This, I do not know, belonged to which category, but dressed in a pair of jeans and a shirt, I found myself padding up. With a major disconnect between my mind and my actions, things seemed to be taking their own course, rather than waiting for my mind to give out any signals for the same.

As I faced the bowler, who was a mild medium pacer, I defended, drove, pulled and cut with equal poise as the cries and yells from the coach subsided with each shot I played. The bowler, who had, till now, been tormenting the previous batsman, now was subjected to the choicest of abuses.

"Hmm... You are not so bad. Which club do you play for and what were you doing here?" he asked again, this time with more cynicism.

"Sir, I don't play for any club. I came here just out of curiosity! That's it!" I explained, a little enraptured at the same time that the coach had found me worthy enough to belong to a club.

"What do you do then?" he asked, discomfited.

"Nothing, I mean I will be doing my MBA in a couple of months."

"MBBA, what is that? I've heard of MBBS but what is this MBBA," he asked, befuddled.

"It's MBA, Sir," I explained again.

"Whatever it is. Doesn't seem anything great," he said, and he seemed to stop abruptly.

After a brief pause, during which he probably mulled over a certain something, he asked me whether I would like to play for the club, making sure that at no time should I feel too self-important.

I, though, was taken aback; I never even saw this coming. Are offers at cricket clubs made so easily? Maybe what he saw was quite good, or the cricketing state of Mohan Meakins Cricket Club was in shambles, just like its infrastructure. With a free itinerary in the next few months, coupled with the love for cricket, I said yes in a microsecond.

"Tomorrow 7 a.m., come with your kit and if you are late, run back from the gate itself," he said, sounding as mean as a man of his age could possibly be.

I learnt the man was called Sharma and no one actually knew what his first name was. He was called Sharma ji by all the players, and he addressed them by any insulting abuse he wished to. That was the norm.

I didn't go to the French school as I'd found something far more appealing, my calling, my eternal love, instead. I had never known that getting into a cricket club would be so easy. How would I have, I thought, seeing how my adolescence was spent in tracing ink on reams of paper, trying to prove to the world how my mental capacity exceeded that of most of my peers?

Forget pursuing another career, there isn't even a second choice if the subjects opted for in your higher secondary are Physics, Chemistry and Mathematics sans Biology. If Biology is opted for, the choice of a career automatically leads you to the art of tearing apart and sewing people's anatomy while having a license to do so.

Better late than never, I thought, as I rode back feeling quite excited. Although my cricketing skills had been appreciated and acknowledged by a coach of probably a not-so-reputed cricket club, it still felt good. With two months still to go before I submitted to the perennial grind of a B-school, I could, for once, play the sport I loved so much, that too at a semi professional level.

As I arrived at the club the next day, I could see a horde of youngsters practicing, and it looked like a proper, full-fledged club for the first time. I felt like an old man as I saw young guys, no less than thirteen years of age to college-going guys, who were not more than twenty-one. Here I was, a twenty-three year old IT veteran amongst these minors. Naturally, I was a little embarrassed -an embarrassment which was initiated by the children there, who started tossing dirty glances at me, like I was a pedophile searching for my prey in a park.

I collected myself as I walked up to the coach and greeted him. He looked at his watch with a frown. "You are five minutes late on the very first day!" he snarled at me as I stood there.

After completing the five rounds of running around the ground, as castigation for coming late, practices commenced. Edginess was pretty evident as I fumbled with the pads for almost ten minutes with a flood of thoughts clamoring for attention in my mind. As I held the bat and occupied the crease, I felt a little calm. All said and done, I had nothing to lose, I reminded myself.

To my surprise, I was by far the fiercest hitter in the club which was obvious by the way everyone gathered around the net I was batting in, whilst I took apart every bowler I faced. Thanks to the countless hours in the gym, with a strong muscular frame, I was bowling quickly too. It didn't take more than a couple of days for everyone in the club to know me.

"What is your age?" the coach asked, four days into practice.

"I am twenty-three," I said.

"Damn, you're too old! Where were you all this time?!" he said, and I took it as a compliment.

"Sir, I never thought that I could play well," I said, honestly.

"Who said you play well?" He spoke like his normal self, making sure that at no point should I feel good about myself.

"I understand, Sir." I said, handing him the upper hand in the conversation again.

"Would you like to play the DDCA under twenty-one tournament that starts next week? Or you are too busy with your MBBA eh?!" he asked, intentionally sprinkling that last acerbic 'eh'.

"But I'm twenty-three, Sir," I said, flummoxed.

"That doesn't matter. Just give me two passport size photographs and you'll be twenty-one in no time," he spoke, quite confidently.

"Thank you, Sir," I said calmly, trying not to betray the happiness I felt at the prospect of being officially a part of a club team now. In no time was a ration card produced which stated that Vineet Grover was indeed twenty-one years of age, a proof, Sharma said, that was more than enough to get me into any under twenty-one team in India.

When he was around, I never needed to say much, as if he understood me. If, for a moment I struggled, he would come up to me, shout out a few obscenities and I never repeated that mistake again. It was strange but despite his arrogance and his foul mouth, I still liked him. He was someone who tried hard to be egotistical and snobbish, like a soldier of yesteryear, proud of his accomplishments. His torso inflated with pride whilst he walked like he was in the army just yesterday, but a man kind enough to help a small kid cross the street if he saw him struggle.

He had a gem of a heart and was venerated by all the children at the club despite the wonderful adjectives they were addressed by. In one particular conversation with the local lads, I came to know that many of the boys, who were from families that could not financially support their cricketing interests, had their requirements sponsored by him. Looking at Sharma, one knew that he was the man who worked hard for the day and had enough money at the end of it to get him one peg of whisky, some food to eat, and a roof to cover his head.

As time passed, I got to know the tragedy that had befallen him. A budding Club cricketer, he got hit by a rising bouncer aimed straight at his unprotected head and eye. He lost one eye during the process and his complete cricketing career came to an abrupt and sad halt. Disappointment transformed into anger as the disgruntled man, with time, turned cynical and cranky. He tried a lot, but to take in his inability to sight the ball was too much for him. He took to drinking and just like the umpteen movies one gets to see, ended up making a mockery of his life.

Finally, after sixteen years of hibernation, he visited the cricket field again to give something back to the game which had taken away everything from him. My respect for him only grew exponentially and every abuse he now hurled at me, I accepted with nothing less than absolute glee.

The DDCA cricket tournament was the time I actually realised my talent was really special. My ability to spot the ball early was what separated me from the normal herd of cricketers; at least this is what Sharma told me, though it was a part of a more elaborate sentence the culmination of which stated that I was a jerk for wasting this special gift.

This hiatus before FMS was a blur as most of the time I found myself practicing. I lost complete touch with the outer world. Surviving on a diet of cricket, I, at times, forgot that I was joining a tier 1 business school in a month. As for the club matches, I was usually the top scorer for my team, which comprised of mediocre cricketers, and I was, by far, the most prolific scorer for my club. With matches scheduled every second day, pain had become a regular sensation in my body. Put an IT bloke into such a grueling schedule, what else could one expect.

Back spasms, muscle pulls, blisters, leather ball blows and a rapid loss of 6 kgs was what I came to within a month into this itinerary. But the sweet joy of scoring runs for your team inspite of the strain your body is being subjected to, is something that cannot be explained. Ask a soldier how the blood dripping from his wound feels, from the bullet he takes upon his chest for his country. Ok, that's taking it a bit too far, but it's the closest that comes to explaining what I felt like.

❖ ❖ ❖

As I had expected, things with Sonali started getting difficult. With this kind of a schedule, I found it extremely difficult to return her calls and messages.

"What is the problem, Vineet?" She asked one day after I returned from practice and called her after seeing multiple calls and messages from her.

"Nothing, yaar. Why do you ask?" I asked nonchalantly, true to what I actually felt.

"Nothing is wrong according to you?! I called up three times and messaged I don't know how many times waiting for your reply, but you are too busy!" she whined.

"Sonali, you know I had a match today. I just got home and called you immediately!" I tried to explain my side of the story.

"I know I know. You and your matches and your cricket. Do I still hold any place in your life?" she asked.

"What kind of a question is that? Of course you do baby," I tried to tone down the irritation in my voice.

"Stop babying me! Things are going horrible between us, in case you do not realise that yourself!" she spoke, quite worked up.

"When did that happen,yaar?" I was candid, since I really did not find anything wrong.

"Oh yes! You didn't. Not a surprise," she said as she cut the call.

Too tired to indulge in courting her, which I was sure would take up the whole night, I let it be. She was right.I was obsessed, maybe too obsessed. Nothing else in my life held importance anymore. Just standing in the field felt so good, irrespective of the blazing 40-plus degree heat. I loved and cherished every moment in the field and when off it, I would longingly think about the game.

Things with Sonali were turning bad and pointed towards one single direction, and despite knowing that, I did not care. She had become over bearing and her whining on the phone had reached unbearable levels. It was a Sunday, a welcome break for me, when I called her. She did not take the call and despite numerous attempts throughout the day, there was no response. At night, a two-line message declaring the break up, beeped. Just as she thought I was being a jerk, my thoughts about her being unreasonable with her attention problems and time-seeking demands had also incepted. It was a strange night, as I recall. I couldn't gather my feelings for what had happened. I wanted to be sad and morose seeing how I had loved her for nearly a year and a half now and her absence made me feel quite hollow and empty. Somehow the hollowness never made me sad. "Did I love her, or was she more of a habit for me?" was the question that I grappled with, throughout the night.

Nevertheless, the habit of love, or whatever it was, faded into the backdrop as my cricket zoomed ahead in full throttle.

❖ ❖ ❖

Ours was a weak team in a league of sixteen, and each team was to play the others once, the Indian Premier league championship format to be precise. We were a club which was used to being in the bottom six or so, at least this is what my fellow team mates told me. Interestingly, there was never an atmosphere of sorrow or self-pity after a defeat, since my team took it as routine. It was an event which was inevitable, something which was meant to be. However, a victory was cherished like none other, something which might or might not come again. The victory ritual was to spend that night at the club practice pitch, along with a lot of alcohol, and everyone got extremely drunk and babbled on about their part in the victory.

Sharma also joined us once in a while, reciting anecdotes from the times he played, drawing parallels to that day's game, talking like a veteran and commenting on how the game had changed over time.

After our third victory, which came in an unsurprising twelve matches, the feeling was that of incredulity. We had beaten the top-seeded team in the league. It was an improbable situation from where the team had won the match. Again, stuck in a situation of familiarity at 32/4, I had paved the way for victory for my team with an innings which falls under the once-in-a-lifetime category. I had pulverized the bowling attack amassing an insane '131 not out' from a mere 63 deliveries.

Although the stadium was empty sans a few grounds men, security guards and a dog, the pat on the backs from the opposition had made me feel ecstatic. In the empty ground, the shrieks and the howls of my team mates had resonated and echoed and there was the craziest display of emotion when we won the match.

For the first time in my sixteen-match long career, Sharma actually smiled at me, a smile which expressed more gratitude than happiness. Here was a man who ran a club with almost no funds and support, was out there just for the love of the game, manufacturing failures year after year, still hopeful of producing that one cricketer, a reflection of his own, in whose success he could find solace and maybe the meaning of his life that remained.

It felt as if he wanted to live his past for once, without the constant feeling of emptiness, without an urge to go out there again and prove a point. He didn't say it but his smile said more than he could have, in his entire lifetime.

It was a bolt from the blue, a surprise that wasn't really welcome because it tore my insides apart. The very next day after my scintillating display of cricket, I was contacted by someone from the Royal Delhi Club, the same club which we had crushed the day before.

In not a very subtle display of player whoring, I was asked point-blank whether I would like to leave that 'shithole' of a club I was currently playing for, and join the elites of the elite Royal Delhi Club, which they said was as tough to get into, as it is to get a seat in a Delhi medical college. There was money on offer for being a semipro as the word 'turn professional' and 'Team Delhi prospects' were used copiously to emphasize the clout the Royal Delhi Club commanded across cricketing circles in Delhi.

In Infotech terms, it was as if the Business Unit head himself called and offered you to move onsite with an unheard-of salary hike. Turning down an offer as alluring as this one was beyond me. Torn, I weighed the pros and cons of either side as I saw myself stacking pro after pro under the Royal Delhi Club tab as the Mohan Meakin side of the argument lay eerily empty.

It didn't take long before Sharma noticed the lost expression on my face. The next day at practice, as my mind grappled with the offer at hand, unable to understand what my next step should be.

"You look out of sorts. What's the matter?" asked Sharma as he literally dragged me by my arm to one side.

"Nothing, Sir. I am fine," I replied, caught unawares.

"No shit, you are not. Are you unwell?" he asked again.

"No, Sir, I am fine."

"Then start concentrating on the bloody drill!" he scowled as he turned back and walked away.

I couldn't stifle my problem any longer and I heard myself calling him back.

"Yes! What now?" he asked irritated.

"I have to talk to you about something, Sir," I spoke, finding it insanely hard to lock eyes with him.

I half expected him to shout back, but he didn't. I looked up to see his expression but I saw him staring blankly at me, unable to understand what it was that I was going to tell him.

As ashamed as I was afraid of mouthing those words, I found myself incapable of telling him the truth.

"Will you say it?" he spoke, politer than his usual self, maybe the lull before the storm, I thought.

"I have been asked by the Royal Delhi Club to join them," I almost whispered, as I made it a point to stare directly at my shoelaces. Expecting a slap at a ferocious pace or an abuse unheard of, I gathered enough courage to covertly eye him.

He stood there unmoving and silent. At a snail's pace, I slowly lifted up my head in an awkward endeavor to make eye contact with him. Before my glance could meet his eyes, I reached his slightly parted lips, which resembled a meek smile. I had heard before, that the epitome of anger is disbelief which is usually characterised and initiated by a sadistic smile. Drawing analogies, I understood that I was indeed in for a humiliation of a lifetime.

"That is good news," he spoke in the softest voice; a voice that I didn't actually believe was his. Never before that day had he spoken in such a cushy manner. He looked like a content man, unlike his usual impatient and snarling self. Oddity struck as I was literally dumbfounded, unable to comprehend what had just come about. I was now staring at him, albeit unintentionally, maybe to find the catch behind his last spoken sentence. Sincerity and solemnity was all I could gather.

"Sir, are you serious?" I questioned out of disbelief, paying no regard to the fact that what he'd said was what I had foolhardily wished for all this time.

"Yes, I am," he said, as his stifled smile gave way to a more generous one.

"You are kidding me right? I am sorry, I shouldn't have asked this," I spoke initiating immediate damage control, almost sure by now that he would snap at me any time.

"Come with me," he said, as he walked slowly, his posture more relaxed than normal, his walk more casual. He walked away from the nets towards a large tree that stood erect at one corner of the ground.

He didn't look back, as I followed him a few steps away, watching the calmest Mr. Sharma I had witnessed in the past month and a half. He settled beneath the shade of the enormous Banyan tree as he signaled me to do the same.

"When I saw you for the first time, I knew you had something in you," he spoke with that same smile which seemed to be permanently fixed on him.

Not knowing what the statement actually meant, trying to put perspective to it, I sat there a little perplexed. Still, I pretended to listen, although my mind raced to draw conclusions to what Sharma was about to say.

"I could see me in you. The same nerve, the same carelessness, yet the same insane amount of talent. Something divine," he said, with a sparkle in his eye that sent goose bumps down my body.

"Thank you, Sir" said I, almost dazed at the compliment he bestowed on me, still the uncertainty lingered.This sounded too good to be true.

"Do you really mean that?" I asked, to be sure.

"Yes, I do," he confirmed, though I was still a tad unsure.

"I am sorry. Now that I sit here and see what I have got from this club, I would be a soulless bastard to let it go for something which seems better at this time," I gushed emotionally..

"No, it's not like that Vineet. Such things..."

"No sir, I know I am wrong, and I feel pathetic for it," I said, interrupting him.

"See, Vineet. You were not out on a social cause. You are here to be a cricketer who may represent India someday. Aren't you?" he asked, launching me into a zone that I hadn't been for a long time. Was being a cricketer my actual dream or was it a far fetched fantasy? Are dreams and fantasies the same? Aren't dreams called dreams because they are never meant to be fulfilled? Why was

Sharma making the fact of being a cricketer sound so casual and trivial?

I think I was expected to say yes to this one and so I did.

"Good, so these are the opportunities you have to grab. Keep your feet on the ground but if some one offers you to touch the sky, you bloody well should do it," he spoke, with the smile wiped off and an expression of intense passion now clearly visible on his face.

"I understand, Sir. So you mean I should... " I couldn't get myself to complete the sacrilegious sentence.

"Yes, you should go ahead. You have no clue what Royal club is. If there is a route to the Delhi team, it is through the club," he explained.

"They have won the last seven championships and that too ridiculously easily, and it's not because they breed the best players, it's because they have so much monetary pull, they poach the best. And I know it's not the best place to be in if morals are considered, but if you are being poached, you sure are a worthy fellow," he said, making me a little queasy and happy at the same time.

I sat with my head hung, trying to cerebrate a decision but I knew it wasn't going to be so easy.

"So, you won't bear any grudge against me." I said without looking up, simultaneously playing with a few pebbles strewn across the ground.

"No, Vineet, never. This club is a lost cause and I know it. I may sound like a braggart but I am here only to provide a tiny pedestal to mostly the not-so-rich aspiring cricketers. I support them as much as I can and if they are good enough, they themselves leave for bigger clubs. This has happened before, so I am used to it, rather it is what I want," he said with an uneasy calmness, uncharacteristic of the man.

"So, you want me to leave?" I asked him like a small child, almost sounding stupid now, after repeatedly being told the same in no uncertain terms, yet, somehow wanting to hear the word no.

"Indeed," was the answer, as he got up, slapping the dirt off his track pants as he left towards the practice area.

❖ ❖ ❖

After completing the season with Mohan Meakins Club, finishing with some more sparkling innings and even finding a mention of my name consistently in a few six-line excerpts in local newspapers, I was still a relatively unknown name across a few of the Delhi clubs.

The very next day after the culmination of the last match, I signed up with the Royal Delhi Club. The name 'royal' did absolute justice to the infrastructure sported by the club -A huge lush ground, with a plush office situated just besides the pavilion. The coach and a number of other men, supposedly specialists at some or the other facet of the game, sported nothing less than Nikes and Adidas gear. With a sprawling area bang in the center of south Delhi, it was a club reserved only for the offsprings of the insanely rich, bureaucrats, politicians and certain men like me who they said were prodigies.

At the same time, college also commenced. The same awesome feeling of being a student again was delightful. This break from the dungeons of that IT hell felt good. It felt nostalgic to be seated in those good old seats listening to wise men talk. I would occasionally doze off as the dialogue became monotonous and soporific. Sometimes I would launch myself into the world of daydreaming, sitting in my lectures, about cricketing exploits at levels ranging from club to national, often to international century knocks at the Lords. I was occasionally jerked into consciousness by the hushed laughter of the class as the teacher stood there looking at me with the most contempt-laden stare ever.

The hope of a new stock of females to ogle upon although, was crushed badly. My class was the worst compilation of the "fairer" sex one could end up with in a single place. Sometimes, when basking in the sun, they reminded me of the umpteen African safaris I had seen on the Discovery Channel.

Owing to the hectic schedule of the frenzied MBA life, the cricket started suffering. The myths like FMS was a chilled-out college were busted with the same ferocity as my ass would, with the truck-load of assignments and other activities that took place ceaselessly without any breathers. Since it was the cricketing off-season, the absence at practices did not attract a lot of censure but I knew this would not be taken lightly once the season began and besides, the Royal Delhi Club's pride would be at stake.

As the burdens of the MBA life increased, so did the practices at the club and I found myself between a sea of choices. Bunking lectures had become a routine, and I found solace in the grilling heat with sun beating down mercilessly rather than the cushiony chairs of my air-conditioned lecture halls. Promising people the grandest of treats if they called out a 'yes' for me during attendance, helped me get a few extra attendance points. I scraped through the semester examinations, somehow managing to clear all my papers, something that came as a shock both to my professors and my peers. I was ranked 57th in a class of 65, a feat unheard-of in my past life academics, but this was all for what lay on the other side of my life, where I was living the inception of a dream.

❖ ❖ ❖

CHAPTER 5

The Dream Takes Flight

"Life is like a library owned by the author.
In it are a few books which he wrote himself,
but most of them were written for him."

— Harry Emerson Fosdick

What on earth was I thinking? My head was killing me. There I was, sitting in an exam hall,soon going to be the alma mater of one of the most prestigious B-schools in India, for which, all I had to do was merely smear the white answer paper for two hours.

My heart, on the other hand, was pounding from the inside, almost ready to spring out of any orifice it could have found. This was it, I knew. If I had to follow my dream, this was pretty much it. There would be no second chances.

Sharma's word stood correct. The Royal Delhi Club had undeniably made the path an easy one. Each of my performances got eyed by people who mattered, and once I was in my element, there was no looking back. I had been selected amongst so many prodigies to be a part of the trials for the 'Delhi Daredevils'.An old leg like me had been preferred over 'young stallions,' something for which the only explanation was that they had seen something in me. Something special, I added to myself.

The trials for the Delhi team started that day, the very day my third semester examinations commenced. In an hour, I was expected at the trials. On one side lay a cushiony life, guaranteeing the comforts of life, an abode in a posh colony in Delhi, a swanky ride, and a life filled with air-conditioned offices.Innumerable client visits would ensue, which would include infinite sleep-inducing team meetings where I would want to do just one thing i.e. bang my head on the table. I had derived my answer; I wanted the other side of life -that of labour, sweat, toil and uncertainties as to whether all this would materialise even into a fraction of what I'd always dreamt of.

The professor had already entered the class, inspecting whether all the minor errands had been completed before the exam started. The hustle stopped as the students wearily moved onto their respective chairs, clearly showing signs of drowsiness caused by the night spent studying. They simultaneously checked their admit cards, pens, pencils, rulers, etc. What they were planning to do with rulers in an MBA exam was beyond me, I had shunned it in class ninth standard itself, I thought.

Rulers can take a back seat, I thought, as I quickly jerked back to the present, where I had a more epochal decision to make. Out of impatience and nervousness, I was twitching both my feet with utter ferocity now. What the hell, I thought, I felt motivated to do the insane as the gut feeling took over. Gathering all my belongings, I stormed past the narrow corridor formed between the lines of adjacent chairs. I glanced over the derivatives paper that I was supposed to start solving in a minute's time and it looked fatally menacing. If there was any hesitation in my step, it vanished that very moment. Bemused, the lecturer started to form a statement, but gave up even before starting off with the first syllable. Why he did that, I still don't have a clue. May be the whole universe was in this conspiration or something.

Before I knew it, I was sprinting towards the parking lot. I collected my kit from the parking guy, something for which I'd pay him ten rupees, and mounted my Bullet. I felt lighter, alive, and for once during this whole episode, it just felt right.

I pumped the kick viciously as my bullet roared. The Delhi air wasn't suffocating anymore, even the intense heat felt light on the skin as I bobbed and weaved through the traffic with a perpetual smile pasted on my face. The sweat under the helmet felt cold now, with the air which my bullet bisected with precision. My mind wandered a bit towards the question paper. Was the question I had learnt by rote by writing it in my notebook 10 times, there? Why had I studied like an idiot the previous night when I could have slept rather nicely for ten hours and could've been fresh, bowling rippers at the trials today?

I couldn't think I was tired, not today, not now, I reminded myself as it was the determining moment of my life, like so many others before -just that this one would make me perennially ecstatic, give me a reason to why I was born, and derive answers to strange questions like why had I held that plastic bat and ball in my teeny hands at four years of age.

I was drenched in sweat by the time I reached the stadium. I ran to the dressing room, had a record-equaling (beating my previous ones) thirty second bath and was in the field within five minutes. My heart sank like the Titanic did on the lamentable day in the

April of 1914, seeing that there were about 100 young men all in whites, with towering physiques, looking mean, all set to be a part of the Delhi team. I inspired myself by thinking of physically huge players who were actually not worth a lot when it came to skill, making me feel better, though only minutely.

Most of these men here had busted their posteriors for years altogether to get here, most of them were merely 12th pass blokes, and I was sure they wouldn't have done it too convincingly either. But who was I to judge them? Atleast they had pursued what they loved, not given into societal pressure of being the next Einstein. On the other hand, I was an MBA grade from FMS, a computer engineer who had worked for Infotech Ltd., who, till 12 months back, used to play mostly with a rubber ball. It sure was a dream, but it would mean nothing if it ended here amongst these 100-odd men, most of whom were as anonymous as I was, and were fighting for the same coveted Delhi slot.

I was frantically looking for the Sehwags and the Gambhirs, but learnt that they did not come to the trials. Of course, I thought, I never attended the Personality Development Programmes at Infotech Ltd. This list would be cut down to a 30 in a month's time and that would be the thirty probables for the IPL. Out of these 30, 10-odd places would indisputably already be fixed, for they would be the Delhi national team regulars and added to that would be the 5-odd mandatory slots for foreign players, which made the total of 15.

The implication of this was that this battle was for the last 15. 1 in every 7, I did quick math, and started looking for jackasses amongst this testosterone-filled congregation. I found quite a few teeny weenies, I'd be better than them, I thought, in a quest to feel more confident.

Majority of this current lot had played the Ranji Trophy some time or the other, either for Delhi or some other state or had been in the extras, bringing in water during the drinks break. The bottom line was that they had been associated with cricket for a reasonable amount of time now. Yours truly, on the other hand, had been writing code and solving complex math and logical problems hardly a year prior to this. "Some jump," I chuckled to myself.

The club level, as I recalled, was easy. Pedestrian breed of bowlers, the most placid of pitches and huge scoops of luck had seen me here. Usually prodigies of sixteen-seventeen take this route and here I was, a twenty-three year laggard, moving up the ladder the same way some of the big players across the cricket world did.

I was lost in my own melee of thoughts when I heard a humongous man, probably 6 feet 5, with the sternest of faces and the most piercing black eyes, shout in thick Haryanavi accent.

"Stand in rows of ten, boys."

The voice complemented his built perfectly and no one would have dared disobey such a man, at least I wouldn't have. His hairline was receding and whatever was left of his hair was combed back perfectly to reveal a huge forehead. He had a bushy moustache and his traps were as huge as a wrestler's. He wore a shining track suit and stood erect, rather too erect for his age which bordered on fifty. I didn't understand why, but few of them started assembling height-wise like during the assembly sessions back in school.Probably they had attended too much school, two, three years in each class, I thought smugly, albeit feeling ashamed at my thought-process and simultaneously appreciating my own sparkling educational background.

Eight rows of ten people were finally formed and four players were left in a last incomplete row, which was then disintegrated and they were then told to join the first four rows. I felt a little elated as the initially discomfiting figure of a 100 was already down to 84.

The monster of a man introduced himself as Pratap, our physical trainer, at the same time boasting not so subtly how he had trained many a hundred back in the National Defense Academy, the breeding ground for the best army officers in the country.

Pratap was accompanied by another man, Prakash, who seemed to be in his early forties, adorned witha rotund belly but a taut posture coming from years of hard work at a physical chore, which I assumed was cricket. He looked a little less imposing than Pratap, a feat which wasn't very difficult to manage knowing how insanely huge Pratap was. Prakash also donned the same pair of track pants but wore a white t-shirt on top, which read Delhi in a grayish-black shade. He was no taller than 5 foot 10 and didn't invitea second glance initially, standing next to Pratap, but immediately grabbed our attention the moment he uttered the first words.

"You are the best eighty-four cricketers in the national capital of a country boasting of more than a 100 crore people, not a mean feat by any measure, guys," said Prakash, suddenly making me feel this sense of achievement. I actually had done something not so ordinary, I reflected.

"But for me that is a shit of an achievement. After the end of this month, there shall only be 15 men who would be in that list which reads Delhi National Team at the top and the rest of you will go back to your clubs to start all over again to be here next year. In other words, this is THE place, guys. Either you put in every iota of strength, every grain of talent and every minute of your day into this game, or you shall be amongst those losers who would be going back. Do not disappoint me. Even if you lose, lose like a winner!" he ended with a flourish.

It reminded me of all the movies in which the coaches give spine-stinging speeches and get their teams to do the impossible. I secretly wished I was the only one who would have heard this awe-inspiring piece of brain food, otherwise now everyone would be equally inspired and hence nullify my inspirational surge. Too much physics in my heydays, I cursed myself.

The players were segregated on the basis of the skill they claimed to possess and the practices started. I came under the all-rounder bracket along with twenty-one other gentlemen. Not a very soothing sight when I knew that there was a spot for one, maximum two all-rounders in the team.

I was made to bat first and there were some seriously quick blokes around. Some had run-ups that could make you break into a cold sweat that very moment. The same conundrum I put up with whenever I face a quick bowler besieged me -whether I should play the way I know, i.e. aggressively, thereby accentuating the risk of losing my wicket, or should I showcase my solid defense, something which I never really possessed.

Better safe than sorry, I thought, was the correct manner to go about things to establish my batting prowess. One after another, bowlers bowled in a round robin fashion and most of them were in the 120-130 kmph category. There was this one lad who was clocking 135 kmph and I was already having problems defending him. All the deliveries I faced from him were either missed, hit my pad or were defended in an ugly manner. I was up against it, I knew it. Obviously, club cricket was all about cute bowlers bowling full length, beckoning me to free my arms, my U.S.P. I was adept at depositing them over the boundary rope, time and again. On the contrary, if I faced an express bowler, I quietly sneaked singles or let the deliveries pass. Here the equation was different; most of these men who would make it to the final 15 would be above a 135 and a makeshift technique to face genuine quick bowling would no more be an option.

With these thoughts cluttering my mind, one 137 kmph delivery crashed into the off-stump. I looked like a fool with the gap between the bat and the pad big enough for Pratap to go through it. I was told to give way to the next batsman and take rest before facing spin. Seeing the sorry state of my defense against genuine pace, I drifted away into my thinking zone. Was I really sane? I mused. Where on one hand I was supposed to be solving balance sheets and doing capital investment analysis, I was here amongst this group of ruffians trying to outdo them at something they'd spent their whole life doing. A delicate city boy who had spent the last two years on cushiony chairs and AC offices barring a brief stint at club cricket was now competing for a slot for the Delhi Daredevils. Not really sane, was my answer after a SWOT analysis.

"Oye! Go there. Your turn to play the spinners!" said a batsman who I guess had his share of spin.

Spinners were bowlers I really relished. Lobbing the bowl up and asking to be hit, well that's what most of them did. The wily ones always gave me some problems here and there but I guess I must have managed all right, that's why I was there in the first place. The catch was that the standard here was many more notches above that of the club level. The pacers were fiery, the spinners got that extra purchase and the batsman had watertight defenses. I had to keep reminding myself that I was no schmuck either.

The grueling day finally got over. If I had to honestly rate my performance it was sub-par and if teams had to be formed from these eighty-four lads, I would probably make it to the fifth team. Few players had already impressed Pratap and Prakash and they had clearly made what is called the 'first thumping impression.' With my head hung low I went back to the locker room. Naked men all around, not exactly what you want to see after a screwed-up day. I gave the bath a miss and plodded back to my bike. My cell had 13 missed calls, mostly from my classmates who must have wanted to ask what on earth had befallen me that I missed the derivatives exam.

I hadn't told anyone about this since I wasn't sure of their reactions. I didn't want my decision to be even remotely influenced by what these money-hungry, morally ransacked tomorrow's nincompoop managers thought, they would never understand what passion is. They had sold their souls just like me to get in this mad rat race to be the best CEO; I, at least, had the guts to try what I actually loved. This fake satisfaction kept me from breaking down. I wanted to call Sonali, tell her everything about how I wasno good at this sport, hung hopelessly in a situation of so close yet so far, but that would have been a purely self-seeking decision, hence I never did. I called up Hardik and blabbered my heart out, all of which he listened to, quietly. I ranted like a small boy as to what a disappointment I had that day, that the dream was over even before it came out of its cocoon, and I would now embrace sanity and do what any pragmatic person would do. I would study and give the rest of my papers and never take to this wretched game again.

"Vineet, what an idiot you are!" laughed Hardik."Who told you to show your lame defense,you asshole? What are you good at? What is it that you did to be here?" he asked."Hit the daylights out of the bowlers, didn't you? That's why you are different from the rest and not because you can defend like Rahul bloody Dravid!" he was almost scowling by now after answering his own question.

"And next time you cry over that lame MBA of yours, I'll personally come down to Delhi and kick your whiny ass. Now go eat something and sleep. Tomorrow show your Pratap what my friend is actually capable of," he ended the conversation just like Shahrukh Khan in Chak De! India.

I thanked him for his tirade to which he retorted that I was turning into a girl and should stop consuming estrogen tablets.

I couldn't sleep for a long while that night, mulling over my destiny. Was this really meant to be or was this yet another one of God's ploys to make easy things difficult for me? Was I meant to be a future marketing guru or a swashbuckling middle-order Michael Hussey for Delhi? The more I pondered on it, the deeper I felt I was mangled in this quagmire of questions. Somewhere in these questions, maybe, I found the reason to sleep, which I thankfully did.

I got up early and had a good breakfast as was suggested by Hardik to keep me going the whole day of intense physical labour. Somehow, I felt more resolute. I made myself a few promises. I swore to myself that even if I was the worst performing player in those 84, I would, under all circumstances, complete the selection camp and then if rejection was handed out, I would accept it, but I would not resign myself to my fate. My second promise to myself was that even if I was laughed at while batting, called a slogger, an empty-headed hoicker, I would still stick to what I knew best.

While making these promises en route to the stadium, something inside me made me stop at the Gurudwara. Atheism can take a back seat, I thought. I knew that God knew that I was being selfish, but he was above all this, it's his incumbency to give and mine to ask, I reasoned to myself. I gobbled up the prasad prepared in dollops of ghee and rode to the stadium. Just like always, I felt immense peace now. Psychological or for real, something inside felt right.

The next few days weren't very special either but I stuck to my basics. The week finished on Friday and we were given a two-day hiatus to recuperate from the draining week. I was more confident of myself now, though with the same issue of extreme pace still haunting me. As luck would have it, Hardik was flying down from Pune, for a week-long vacation to Delhi. Delhi was his hometown and he claimed he was coming to see his parents but the genuine reason was to inject me with that final shot of confidence which I was seriously short of, clearly apparent from my insecure conversations with him on the phone. He never said that he was coming to see me, I just knew.

We met up over beer at my favourite place in Delhi, Howzzat. As the name suggests, it is a place dedicated to the hallowed game of cricket. The décor there manifests cricket in everything one can possibly point out. Every entity there is shaped as a cricket accessory; posters and pictures of venerable cricketers on the walls, the sofas like hand gloves, table-tops mounted on wickets, plates like half-cut bowls, etc. For two cricket junkies whose staple food was beer, this was a temple where the rest of their lives could have been spent, only if there were no financial constraints.

After the initial talks about which females our common acquaintances had been going out with in the past one year, we got down to discussing cricket. I told him how I felt that there was no way on earth I was going to make to the coveted 30 if I kept getting my stumps dislodged five times a day by the speedsters there. To top it off was the concern that if those guys were troubling me at a speed of mid one thirties, what would happen once the speed guns clocked 150s at the IPL, if I ever played one?

"Beta, don't worry, daddy is here," he stated, after chewing peanuts the entire time I was talking.

He said he had a plan for me and I should get ready for the most grueling time of my life. He told me that Sunday morning I was supposed to pick him up at 9 a.m. a long with two of his mates and that we were going to practice. I kept enquiring as to what it was he was up to, but not once did he mention anything. He just sat there with a wry smile glued to his face the whole time.

It was Sunday, 8:30 a.m. and I was in no mood to get up, but I knew Hardik wasn't the one to be messed with. So with a heavy heart, I ruined the only holiday I had in the week. We drove down to a different place than the stadium I had expected, a small Delhi Development Authority sports complex near where Hardik stayed. His two friends were supposed to meet us there itself, and the moment I saw their giant frames, I realised that the day would be harsh.

We moved towards a cement pitch and I could already sense that things were not getting any prettier. Stumps were positioned at the batsman's end and then came the rudest shock. Hardik started walking, counting steps which usually are twenty-two denoting twenty two yards, and he stopped at eighteen. A single stump was placed there signifying the bowling end. The lump in my throat was pretty visible by then. Then came out the heaviest rubber balls from Hardik's bag, which looked pretty innocuous till then.One of the monster lads had brought in a bucket of water at that point.

What in the world?! I thought, now were they going to strip me naked and baptise me to give me special powers to face the hurricane that was about to follow? That would have been better than what actually happened. The balls were first soaked in water, then taped with black electrical tape to make them almost as heavy as a leather ball. May be a bit more. Even Venkatesh Prasad would have been spewing venom if these rockets were handed over to him. The final nail in the coffin was when the bucket of water was poured on the cement pitch. It was official, I was going to die that day, I trembled.

"Go, get padded up, asshole, these rubber balls can rip out the flesh of your body and for once, I am not joking," said Hardik, who seemed to be suffering from a multiple personality disorder at this point in time, his alter ego was surely that of Hitler.

I fumbled into my kit with patches of perspiration now clearly visible across my jersey. Water soaked taped bullets were now being hurled at me at velocities unheard of. The first three went past me in a jiffy, and the best I could offer to them was admiration. Just when I thought I'd see this storm by – till the balls and the pitch both dried up and the balls could be seen again – Hardik went over to Monster No. 2 and told him something in a muffled voice, after which both of them shared a cunning laugh.

Getting a clue as to what they might be up to, I was hoping against hope that it shouldn't be bodyline, not from eighteen yards for God's sake, but instincts seldom fail you. It was a delivery which was pitched at a good length, after which I lost the sight of it and the next thing I experienced was a shooting pain in my rib cage area. It felt as if someone had stabbed me in the lungs and refused to take the weapon out.

The bat fell out of my hands involuntarily and I squatted down, breathing heavily. I knew rubber balls could hurt, but now I knew they could numb you.

"Get up you asshole, is this how you'll make it to the Delhi Dareveils?" Hardik seemed to enjoy this and all I wanted to do was to kick him in the balls.

Over the next two hours, the pitch was wet frequently and the balls were soaked with an even higher frequency. My eyes got used to these screamers, but my batting instincts did not. Everytime the ball hit me, there was this screaming pain that made me want to bludgeon the bowler with my bat. But deep down I knew, the more I sweat here, the less were the chances that I'd get my head blown off in a real game.

Two hours later I was as battered and bruised as a pugilist, just out of a Muay Thai match, like one who had somehow managed to survive the mauling by a guy ten times his size and fifty times his agility. I ended up with my rib cage and groin area crimson red, throbbing with blood clots and surging pains that could not be described in mere words. I felt like I was two people in one, one side purely normal like that of an ordinary man, and the other one swollen like that of a mythical monster. I swear I could see my center of gravity shift towards the left side of my body, yes, it was that swollen.

The rest of the day was spent in icing the swelling and discussing the game with Hardik.

"Jokes apart, by the end of the day I swear you were at least touching half the balls, and trust me, one week of this training and you'll find your Mr. 135 a joke," explained Hardik and he made sense. If you could crack CAT you'd always find other exams a joke, I drew analogies in my mind.

The next week drained me of every ounce of energy I had. After the daily practice sessions, Hardik would come to pick me up and after a 15-minutes car ride to the sports complex, I'd again practice with the two monsters for another couple of hours, under lights, that is. I, myself, could notice the difference in my abilities, as the same deliveries which I could merely get a whiff of, on the first day, were now being stroked quiet well. The ability was there, I felt, the practice lacking, which was now being overcompensated for.

To avoid mental and physical burnout, I would go home, have a good meal, take a hot water shower and straightaway hit the sack. Thanks to this rigorous regime I was forced into by Hardik, by the end of the second week, I had sized up most of the bowlers including Mr. 135.

Rumour had it that any day now, we would have a surprise intra camp match, which would be felicitated by the owners of the Delhi Daredevils and they'd get to have a look at the talent pool at their disposal. With two and a half weeks over I knew this day was lingering around, and I also knew that this was the D day. CAT exam, FMS interview days were now passé, my newest most crucial day could arrive any moment. I had missed all eight of my exams by this time and I was unofficially a whole semester behind my batch mates. Some inspiration! I thought.

❖ ❖ ❖

On the Friday of the third week, the moment I stepped into the stadium, I knew this was the day. The nets had been removed, the boundaries had been laid, the pitch had been rolled over well and a section in the east stand had been adorned just enough to give us an idea about the importance of the people who would witness the game from there. The degree of decorations surey made it clear that they were the people who mattered.

What we were unsure of was how eighty-four players would be made to play a game on the same day and this doubt was instantly laid to rest by Prakash.

"As you can see, today we have the surprise match lined up. Mr. Nagpal and Mr. Malhotra both shall be here in an hour. I am picking out the twenty-four players based on the performances in the last two weeks and of course your previous Ranji and club performances and these would be the players who would play the match today. Others do not lose heart as this is no indicator of the final 30. Let us have a fair and a fighting game."

Yeah right, I thought. If my name is not there in this list, it's signed, sealed and delivered for me. If I cannot make it into this top twenty-four then I would have to get Mr. Sharma laid with Angelina Jolie to make it into the top fifteen all of a sudden. The list was to be announced in another five minutes and each moment of those five minutes was like an eternity in itself. I was sweating like a pig as I always did when nervous. I emptied my bladder twice and had mentally readied myself not to hear my name in that list of twenty-four.

Twenty names had been announced, my heart was now beating at the fastest rate possible. It wasn't as if I was expecting a call, it's just that since this was something I had yearned for, a fake faint little flame of hope still flickered deep down inside.

"Ashish, Vinesh, Sanjit and Kedar." announced Prakash as the last four names. The writing was on the wall. I was officially a loser, as Prakash would put it. Somehow, this time, unlike my usual self, I didn't feel anything. I was calm in an instant, assuring myself that this was never meant to be. Maybe, I read all the signs wrong and hence treaded the wrong path. All the cues that I felt pointed towards me being a cricketer were nothing but a fallacy. The only physical consequence of this shattering piece of news was a sudden brutal pain in my stomach. I somehow staggered back to the dressing room and quietly sat in a corner hoping to weather this storm out. The pain just did not subside.

Finally, after sometime, I let a tear roll down my left cheek. I had thought I was calm this one time and that I had learnt to accept denials. Apparently, I hadn't. The shattering combination of rejection and physical pain by now had set this avalanche of tears perpetrated by the first one that I let out on will, the one I had control over. But after that, tears started rolling down uncontrollably and somehow as each tear left the periphery of my eye, I felt lighter. It was like a load I had carried all my life and someone was helping unburden me, without my consent. Instinctively, I flung all my clothes and stripped down to my boxers. I ran to settle down under a shower, crying, trying to get rid of all the tears I could possibly muster, so that never again should I come to this.

Once I felt I had emptied the lacrimal gland, I stumbled out of the shower, still not being able to ingest what had just hit me. The tears had stopped but the despair had started increasing exponentially as the truth kept getting entrenched deeper in my mind with every minute. Torn, and mentally dilapidated, I got dressed and left. This would amount to sacrilege, if someone saw that I was missing just because I wasn't selected in one of the teams.

But no one would care about such a non-entity on such an important day, I convinced myself. For once, I knew even alcohol couldn't mollify my pain, only time could.

All day I sat brooding, sipping on a coke and watching something on TV which was more to fill up the eerie quiet, mentally disturbing ambience with pictures and sounds, all of which was obviously of no meaning to me as my mind was cluttered with questions to which I had no answers.

I had this urge to talk to someone. Hardik was out of the question, the poor guy had specially flown down to help me get my act right and I had failed him miserably. Sonali came to mind again and so did my self-centeredness of remembering her only when I was in dire need of a loved one, whereas during times of normalcy I hardly remembered her. Somehow, I summoned up enough shamelessness to buzz her.

"Hi Sonali."

"Hi Vineet."

"How are you?" I was talking to her after six months, and listening to the sweetest voice on earth wrenched my heart.

"I am good. How are you?"

"I am good..., well not so good. Just wanted to talk to you for some time," I said, in a horribly pitiful voice.

"Yes, go ahead," she said in her super-mellifluous voice but the sternness in it was pretty perceptible.

"First I just want to say I am sorry for what..." I had just begun when I was interrupted.

"Please Vineet. Let's not go there. It took me three months to get over you, while you didn't give a damn and I do not wish to be reminded of that phase again. If you want to share something other than your feelings, it's OK, but for your feelings about me, it's too late for that!" she exclaimed.

She was right, I knew deep down, but somehow the image of her in my mind was still that of a fawning girlfriend who's long distance complains had become overbearing and had forced me to call it quits. I had pushed away someone who loved me so much, just like that. Just like something I loved the most kicked me today. Ironical as it was, I wish I had the courage to laugh at the situation but it pained so much that I couldn't.

"I understand Sonali. It's just I'm sorry for everything," I concluded, with my voice cracking several times in that last sentence as I hung up the phone. I was half expecting her to call back, just to enquire, just to listen to me, just to help me out in the most pathetic phase of my life, but she didn't and I could not blame her for that, not even a wee bit.

Misery aggravated through the night and forget being able to sleep, I did not even try to close my eyes. With my left half still swollen, a reminder of the futile hard work I had put in, I felt like a fool. Who said hard work never goes to waste, well it just did and it hurt, both mentally and physically, I thought.

I had two options, either to regroup and face the music starting Monday, very evidently for no reason other than getting whatever ego I had left, be destroyed by Pratap and the coach, or pull myself out of this fantasy world back to the real one where I was supposed to be an MBA from a tier 1 B-school.

If skipping the exams was a big decision, this time I was facing a mammoth one. It was regarding my summer internship, where B-school graduates are supposed to work for two months with a professional organisation to gain industry exposure, which began that Monday onwards. I was placed with Holden Partners, a top rung management consulting firm, something for which most of my batch mates would literally kill me. My initial plan was to cite health reasons for being late to join the firm, that is, if I was kicked out of the camp. Though, if I was selected amongst the 30 probables for the Delhi Daredevils then every Holden Partner collectively in the world could go to hell from my side. I had chuckled at the mental disdain I felt for the firm.

But waiting another week to listen to what manifested everything that had happened at the selection camp in the past three weeks would have been extremely preposterous. I would rather go to Holden Partners the very first day, lick asses, which was supposedly the fastest way to climb the corporate ladder and get myself a Pre-placement offer, the compensation package for which was an astronomical sum, another thing for which my batch mates would kill me for, may be even twice.

Wound in this conundrum, I wondered what I should do next and this time there was no Hardik and no Sonali to guide me through. I so wanted to talk to dad and mom at this point in time, but that wasn't an option either.

It was a Sunday night and I found myself ironing my formals for the next morning. My induction was to begin at 9 a.m. at the Taj Hotel, Delhi, where the CEO and other head honchos of Holden Partners would be coming to welcome the new line of potential future consultants at their firm. The rest of my life would be spent in 5-star hotels ordering exotic food, swimming in unbelievably blue swimming pools, accepting Black Label from the prettiest damsels in business class flights, flying to picturesque places and A.C. offices at commercial hubs of the world like Delhi,

Mumbai, Singapore, New York, etc.

On the other hand, there was misery, dejection, ego blasting, blood, sweat, pain and what I feared most—rejection, the probability of which almost neared one. Undecided, I lay on my bed, trying not to think of the selection camp anymore. Holden would be my life from now onwards and I should accept it. Making myself assimilate this fact, I fell asleep.

I still do not know what metamorphosis my mind underwent during those eight hours of sleep. Divine intervention, I suspect. I got up as if there was no dilemma to begin with. I thought no more and found myself packing for practice again. I remembered one of my two pronged oaths, which stated that I would complete the practice no matter what the signs were.

I quickly mailed the HR stating jaundice as the reason (once again) for my inability to attend office for the induction period of a week, and that I was in the recovery phase and would join "ASAP." Along with the mail, I bid goodbye to my 18 lakh p.a. PPO. Consultants don't hire unprofessional people who suffer from illness on the most important days of their lives.

At the camp, the last week zoomed by, quicker than any other, both because I had now stopped worrying about the outcome and because I was playing just for the love of the game. Everyone except the elite 24 had stopped practicing like mad dogs now. On the other hand, the battle for the coveted 15 slots had intensified amongst the elite 24. It was fascinating to see one elite-24 face another. The grunt let out at the end of the delivery of one elite-24 was an indicator how badly he wanted that slot and the intense concentration with which the batsman tried to dispatch it, showcased his compelling desire to make it to the squad. I, though, just wanted to plunder every delivery out of the ground and bowl mean bouncers to the elite-24, just for kicks and just to prove it to myself that I was as good if not better. I got the occasional stares and swears but with nothing at stake, I never gave two hoots.

Friday was the Judgement Day, when the team was to be announced. On my way to the stadium I had this internal voice coaxing me to stop at the Gurudwara once more. The uncalled-for, rational me questioned its use , citing the last visit as a complete failure, but my upbringing which entailed remembering God all the time, at least during the most critical junctures in your life somehow made me stop there and offer a quick prayer. I put in 500 Rupees, a huge amount for a student, in the donation box, and left. I had this despicable feeling of trying to bribe God to get me a place in the team, something I felt even God might also not be able to manage now, but I got over it soon enough as more important issues like the final team selection list and my Holden Partners internship fiasco cluttered my mind.

The stadium was unusually quiet that day, with the atmosphere eerily anxious, something which had spread like a contagious disease. One felt as if it was a day of mourning and the slightest of noises would disturb this still environment, so no one took the chance. Pratap and Prakash, who were usually there before time were nowhere to be seen either. The elite 24 had a complicated expression which came across as smug to my gang, i.e., gang of 'losers' and fraught with queasiness to the rest of the elite 23.

After an hour-long wait, we saw the six feet five inch Pratap and the corpulent coach along with a man dressed in a jet black suit. He looked like he'd headed straight out of a Hollywood movie where he just played a CIA agent, and then drove his Black SUV with panache on his way here. He wore black Ray-Bans that concealed his eyes, the last source of expressions on his otherwise expressionless face.

The three of them came and stood before us, when Mr. CIA's unyielding face gave way to a mild smile.

"Good to see all you guys here, till the last day, fighting it out for a contract with the Delhi Daredevils franchise. I am the Chief Executive Officer of the franchise, Pankaj Jaiswal. As you all know, today is the day when 15 amongst you will be selected for the franchise. The rest 15 are composed of known faces from the Indian national team and foreign players. Before announcing the names, let me congratulate all of you for making it this far, and I believe everyone here is as good as the other and we had a super tough time selecting only 15 from this supremely talented group of cricketers."

It would really have been tough in that Armani suit and the black SUV, I thought.

"Well, Mr. Prakash, please read out the names," demanded Mr. Jaiswal, albeit politely.

Although, at this point in time, it should have been an unbelievably tense atmosphere, it actually wasn't. The elite twenty 24 who had subconsciously or consciously occupied an area close to each other were the only ones probably crapping their track pants. It didn't matter to me of course, who all got selected. By the time ten names had been called, none of them aberrations from the expected, an unexpected and uncalled-for urge to hear my name emerged. I knew it was impossible but who can explain logical things to that tiny little ticker below the left lung? 13 names gone. Please God, please, somehow, something, please, I almost begged incoherently in my mind.

"Vaibhav Mehrotra," the coach muttered, a far cry from the way he had been shouting names till now.

Holy mother of God, I thought and probably so did everyone else in that ground. It was the super loser spinner whose every legitimate delivery he would ever bowl in his career could be hit for a six. Vaibhav was short, fat, unfit and the best job for him would be that of a clown at a circus. We had wondered about his selection even for the camp, but with time no one paid much heed to it, as for us, he was a non entity, except that he drove a Porche. After the initial shock, everyone mentally concluded that this miracle was a result of a few political strings Vaibhav or his kin might have pulled.

The fifteenth name also was a surprise, a mediocre all-rounder called Sandeep, who was nowhere close to being good enough for the Delhi Daredevils, but now maybe even private companies had started the quota system, I reasoned.

By now, I had stopped feeling sorry for myself and felt worse for the two deserving lads whose positions had been gobbled by Vaibhav and Sandeep.

"These are the 15 most deserving candidates and I congratulate them once again for being a part of the Delhi Daredevils team," Mr. Jaiswal ended.

Duh!

"Anyhow, enough gloom, we have a party at Mr. Nagpal's farmhouse at Gurgaon today, hope to see you all there. There'll be lots of booze and beauties for all of you. Let's celebrate, and best of luck for your future!"

With the speech ending on this high note, he felt he had played the part of a perfect orator, with the right mix of emotion, inspiration, declaration and finally, happiness and hope. The CIA agent then gracefully turned and left with his entourage following him, two odd steps behind.

There were subtle high-fives amongst those selected followed by a bunch of handshakes from the loser clan to the selected ones. To my amusement, no one congratulated Vaibhav or Sandeep, making it clear to them that when it came to us, we appreciated only hard work and real talent and not string-pulling bastards.

Having made only acquaintances and no real friends in the past one month here, I had nowhere to go. I really wanted a chilled beer, but had no one to share it with. My college mates were all busy with their internships, which I was missing with no apparent guilt or remorse. I was fine giving Holden and my one lakh a month stipend a miss, not a very natural thing for an MBA to do, but was I even one?

I went to a 'Chilled beer and wine shoppe' and picked up a couple of Budweisers and rode back home. My place was surprisingly empty and quiet as I recall. It didn't take long to don upon me that it was my inner self that I was super imposing on the physical attributes of my place. I felt utterly depressed having screwed up every possible cardinal event in my life-Sonali, FMS, my internship and now a chance to be with Delhi Daredevils. The buds filled some part of this emptiness and the rest of it was filled by a pizza from Domino's. Once the pints acted up, I fell asleep with the sound of the TV acting as the lullaby for the night.

CHAPTER 6

The Party

"Grief can take care of itself, but to get the full value of a joy you must have somebody to divide it with."

— Mark Twain

I got up fresh, feeling much lighter. Finally after ages, I was not stuck on a crossroads, pulling my hair out not knowing which path to take. I had a definitive path, that of pursuing my MBA and to do it properly and with all my passion. No more dreams would I chase, like a mad dog chasing a car which most of the times is an exercise in futility. To top it off, if the dog has rotten luck, it gets squashed to a messy concoction of bones and pulp, spending its last breath, mangled, under the tyre of a car. I was not that dog anymore, I thought satisfactorily.

Another two days till my life falls into place, when on Monday I'll step into the Holden office, beckoning glances, being a slim and trim, full-haired attractive looking gentleman, a rarity in the corporate world. I'll lick all the asses I missed in the first week and spend my entire two months selling my soul to the devil for the company. They shall be obliged to "PPO me."

Since life would be sane again, I was now mentally at peace. With nothing else to do, I thought I'd visit the party hosted by Mr. Nagpal that night, have some free Johnny Walker Black Label, meet the likes of Virender Sehwag and Gautam Gambhir and if I was lucky enough, I might be coming home with a nice bootylicious party cougar, a new term I discovered denoting the women at a party looking for a one- night stand with young eligible men like me. The utter loneliness in my life had incited this thought-process in me, I figured. If not mental comfort, I was ready to replace it with physical pleasure. Dressed in a black shirt and blue jeans, I smothered myself with my Calvin Klein perfume and promised myself that I would try and have a nice time and not think about the morning. Farmhouse parties in Delhi are undoubtedly the best parties you can be at, in terms of the chunkiest melt-in-your-mouth grilled chicken, freely flowing imported scotch and girls with super-malleable morals. I guess the term stinking rich was coined after someone attended a farmhouse party and the combination of scotch, grilled meat and oodles of expensive perfumes let out this noxious stink.

Sometimes these parties make you sick in the stomach. The shameless show of wealth, unprecedented wastage and swanky pretence build up to the point that it makes you nauseous. This farmhouse party was no different; all of the aforementioned was in plenty. Booze, bimbos and buffet, as some young brash kid would like to put it.

There were present the ugliest of men dressed in expensive clothing and surrounded by expensive wives. I call them expensive because other than money I saw no reason why such dazzlingly gorgeous women would even come near the shadow of such ugly men, let alone marry, engage in acts of horror and bear them ugly little offsprings.

Everyone who was in the guests list in this party either came in a Merc, BMW, Bentley or cars which I had only seen in auto-car magazines under the premier section. Only the camp boys like me had come on their bikes, autos or taxis.

The selection camp guys were also there, the ones selected came to celebrate and the ones who weren't, I guess, came to avenge their rejection by indulging in all the expensive liquor they could. I met up with a few of them, who were at best acquaintances to me, and from them I came to know that Mr. Sehwag hadn't bothered to show up at this mad display of ostentatious vulgarity. Good for him, I thought. Not wanting to hang out any longer with 'the gang,' I wanted to be a loner to attract my party cougar. She was supposed to be the predator and I the prey, and prey that roam around in a herd are not hunted upon, I recalled my Animal Planet lessons. So I excused myself, settling comfortably besides the bar, on the lookout for females now.

I was confused whether to look out for twenty-somethings, young, unmarried, difficult-to-get-rid-of-the-next-morning or the initially planned thirty-somethings, married, bored of their tediously unfulfilling sex lives with their overweight, ugly underperforming husbands and with no strings attached the next morning. The latter seemed a better option, that too by some distance. I was trying to zero in on a thirty- something loner like me, who would fill the emptiness in my life by hers, when this familiar posture struck me.

I knew who she was; it was just that the alcohol had slowed down my mental aptitude by this time. She was standing with her back towards me talking to a group of elderly women who seemed to be very enchanted by what she was telling them. I immediately got up from my hunting pedestal and started walking to a position from where I could see her.

Seeing a mere glimpse of her face, I was glad to see it was Simi. She looked much prettier than what she did back in Infotech. Draped perfectly in a dazzlingly black saree, she radiated the aura of a full-grown woman as compared to the childish vibes she exuded back in Infotech. Her figure drew perfect curves and she had put on a little weight, albeit at all the right places. I felt a little ashamed at noticing all this instead of going and saying hello to her first thing.

I waited for the flock of elderlies to leave and at the first moment available, I made an appearance in front of her.

"Oh my God! Vineet! What on earth are you doing here?" she spoke ecstatically with the same radiant smile she always had when she spoke to me.

"Hi Simi! Infact I would have asked you the same question, but I remembered your father was some big shot in Delhi and figured such parties would be daily routine for you," I said, answering my own question.

"Leave all that! You tell me, how come you're here?" she inquired.

"Well, all that and more, once we get a place to sit down and chat," I said.

"Yeah sure, let's get out of here, else there'll be people disturbing us every second," she said, holding my arm and dragging me out of the party.

Curious onlookers, specially the selection camp eighty-four were now eyeing me with their peripheral vision as I followed Simi.

She took out a key and clicked a button, a black BMW 3 series beeped some fifty meters away in the parking lot.

"Jesus Simi!Is that yours?" I gasped.

"Not mine, it's my dad's, okay now it's mine, since he just bought a Bentley," she smiled.

I had known during Infotech days that Simi was rich, but this rich was beyond my comprehendible limits. I had already started feeling a little uneasy by now. I opened the door for her like a chivalrous gentleman and then sat next to her.

"So, where to?"She asked.

"You tell me! I'm full with scotch and chicken anyways."

"Ok, then we can sit here and talk," and she was right, what better than sitting in a BMW, spacious and cushiony as a car can possibly be.

"So now tell me, how come you are here, Mr. Vineet?" she said facing me, glowing, looking devilishly pretty in the scant moonlight falling faintly across half her face. Her lip-gloss emanated a fresh strawberry scent and filled the air-conditioned BMW with faint whiffs of it as she spoke. I could not comprehend why an angel like her had liked a bike-riding relatively penniless guy like me all this time.

"Hello, where are you?" she exclaimed, as she looked at my dazed and drunk eyes, which were unable to take in all this beauty at once.

"Oh!Sorry," I smiled. I began telling her my story, starting with my life at FMS and how I started playing cricket, enrolled for a club and made it to the Delhi Daredevils selection camp. Finally, how the dream had been crushed right in front of my eyes. I found her listening intently and quietly all this while, probably in pity, I thought.

"Awesome, Vineet. You tried to follow something you loved, there is no man greater than a man who does that," she said.

Along with being endowed with so much beauty, she had started talking much more intelligently than the times in Infotech. What had she been reading? I wondered. She consoled me in her soothing voice, explaining how there are just a few people who get within sniffing distance of their dream, and I was lucky to do just that.

"Don't give up hope at this crucial juncture. Who knows, you could make it to the team next year or heck, even this one. You've just given eight odd months to the game and you want everything. It takes time Vineet, anything you love takes time to be yours," she completed.

May be she meant a lot more than what she made it sound like, but by this time I was hardly taking in anything she said, so mesmerized was I with just how elegantly her lips formed words and sentences. The urge became unbearable and I leaned over to place my lips softly on to hers.

She stopped talking, and sat still. Her hand rose and touched my cheek and her eyes closed slowly. After a moment, we leaned into the kiss, which quickly turned from a lingering soft embrace into a passionate hunger for each other. With sometime into the make out session, both of us had lost crucial articles of clothing and the intensity of our passion had increased."I really loved you

Vineet, I did," she said, while in the act, and panting for breath simultaneously.

Not fathoming what she meant completely, I jerked back. Still mostly out of my senses, I sat there with a dumb expression on my face. I didn't love her; we were supposed to be two friends sharing a moment, and drunk enough to give physical pleasure to each other. I thought the feeling was mutual.

"I understand. I'm sorry, how could I forget you've never loved, or heck, even liked me!" she said, in a muffled voice, which broke while she spoke, and I knew what was about to follow.

She started whimpering in a very low tone and in a minute her tears were clearly visible against the moonlight and, my god, they shone like little pearls. Sadistic pleasure, you may call it, but she looked insanely cute, like a tiny baby letting out innocent tears. I hugged her tightly and apologised for what happened.

"You are a special girl Simi, and I am sorry. I do like you a lot but I have never thought of you that way. Today it was the alcohol that made this happen and I apologise for it." I felt sorry for what I had done to such a wonderful girl, I had made a mockery of her feelings. I was covered in guilt when I spoke.

"I think I'll leave now, but I'll make it up to you. Lets meet up tomorrow at CP. We'll have coffee and discuss you this time. Why a BMW-driving super-pretty girl worked with Infotech," I said, making a lame attempt at humour. I think I succeeded when she let out a faint smile while wiping the trail of tears on her cheeks that had disturbed the perfect mascara-laden eyes.

We exchanged phone numbers and I left, not back to the party but straight back home. Reminiscing about what happened; I still could not get all the guilt out of my system, feeling bad about Simi and her feelings for me.

❖ ❖ ❖

We met at the Café Coffee Day at Connaught Place in the evening at around 6 p.m. It had rained just an hour earlier, an unusual occurrence for Delhi in May, but it sure was welcome. The blazing sun gave way to a clear azure sky, and the wet earth emanated the kind of smell which gets your spirits high, regardless of your mood. Suddenly you can see a spring in the step and unnecessary smiles on all and sundry, such is the magic of a mild shower in parched Delhi, where all everyone wants, is to move faster, curse the other, and ready themselves to cut throats the first instance they get.

Anyway, to top the buoyant mood the first showers had put me in, came Simi dressed in a simple white I-shooet and blue jeans, sporting an expensive pair of shades and looking gorgeous. May be it was the weather or may be Simi had really become stunning since I'd last seen her in Infotech.

We exchanged greetings by the way of arched eyebrows and subdued smiles.

"You are looking Phewwww today!" I said, not able to control what I felt for her.

"In a good or a bad way?" Simi asked, actually a little nervous.

"Obviously in a good way, dumbo," I said, invoking a beaming smile across her face.

We took a corner table and ordered two frappés, she took it with chocolate sauce and I, with a scoop of vanilla ice-cream.

"So?" I asked in a general sense, with a grin.

"So what?" she blushed.

Why were we sharing these funny moments, like dating couples do, I wondered and got my act straight.

"I meant, so how come Miss Simi, my friend, landed up with a BMW, or rather the other way round?"

"Ah that, it'll sound very filmy yaar, leave it?" She said, though clearly wanting me to probe further.

"What Simi! Please don't make me prod," I said satiating her.

"Well, it's just that after college, dad asked me to come back home and told me that he'would decide a career for me, may be send me off to USA for an MBA, obviously on donation. I really didn't want that, I wanted to do it on my merit so took up the job I landed up with, in college. Dad even coaxed me to pick up a job in some of the best firms in Gurgaon by using his contacts but I turned them down and joined Infotech," she said with a shrug of her shoulders.

"So how come you are here in Delhi?" I asked.

"I want to write GMAT, and wasn't getting enough time to study at Infotech and not everyone is a genius like you, so I quit. I've got another three months to my GMAT. I just hope I don't screw it up," she said, with a hint of worry marring her flawless face.

"I'm no genius, that jaundice break was when I studied! I never had jaundice dumbo!" I mocked her, albeit in a jocular manner.

"I know that, you dumbo," she said, matter of factly.

"No you didn't, you got a welcome-back cake and a card, if you recall, Miss smart-ass," I commented.

She didn't reply, just smiled. She looked down and started sipping her coffee with strands of hair falling across her face. She looked up for a moment and just said, "It was just a welcome-back card, not a welcome back from jaundice card. I was just so happy."

She immediately looked down again, may be to conceal something her eyes might have given away. I sat there silent, trying to understand her. I felt sad for her and ashamed at myself. Even yesterday, the first chance I got, I had thrown myself on her. Again, the guilt started prickling me and the shame was unbearable. I felt small like never before.

"Listen, Simi, I am sorry for every time I might have hurt you. You are a special friend now. Please look up."

She didn't. I held out my hand to her chin to slightly lift it. I saw them again, a stream of tears which had already reached her lips, glossing them all over again. My heart wrenched, such a cute face has been made to cry twice in a day because of an absolute idiot like me. I pulled my chair closer to hers and held her. We didn't talk for the next half hour and she just sat resting her head on my chest. The waiter got the bill citing shamelessness on both counts of me hugging her in public and sitting without ordering anything to eat for such a long time. I paid, and we left. The weather outside had gotten even better than before, and unconsciously we both started taking a walk. I never realised when we held hands till Simi clutched it tightly when thunder struck. Time flew past as Simi let out her usual self, a flurry of stories one after the other, some hilarious; some not so much, but I enjoyed her company nevertheless.

At around 9, we parted ways; I hugged her goodbye and promised to meet up soon. Fraught with mixed emotions, I wondered if I'd started liking Simi or was it just that I had found a known comforting face after such a long time whom I could confide in. Grappling with this emotional turmoil I reached home to gear up for the new life that lay ahead, that of a management consultant. Not very exciting, but isn't that how lives of normal people like mine are, I consoled myself.

❖ ❖ ❖

The mind-numbing beeps of my cell phone alarm jolted me out of my deep sleep the next morning, once again reminding me of those god forsaken Infotech days as I shuddered at the mere thought of going to office. The five times more monetary compensation I would be getting here when canvassed against what Infotech offered, was some consolation. I quickly dressed-up in formals, ready to embrace this new life that lay ahead when my cell phone rang, indicating a number unknown to it.

"Hello?" I said.

"Hello, is that Vineet?" Enquired a raspy voice from the other side.

"Yes, this is Vineet, may I know who's calling?" I said with a hunch that something might have gone horribly wrong. No God no, not at Holden, I prayed.

"Hi, this is Yash Shekhawat from Delhi Daredevils. I am the Secretary to the CDO."

What the hell? I thought. What on earth was happening? I felt a sudden rush of blood surge to my head.

"I have called you up to inform you that you have been selected for the 30 probables as one of the players from the initial list is out due to injury. Is that fine with you?" He asked with no expression in his voice, a firm voice demanding an immediate response.

"Yes,Sir, this is fine, I mean it's great news… and… and... Sir, thank you…this really means a lot… sir, when, I mean where and when do I have to report?" I stammered my reply, like a fifteen-year old asking out an elder woman. Usual to my physiological self, my crisp new shirt was drenched in sweat as I perspired profusely, but what sweet sweat I thought, the feeling was surreal.

"Report at the Feroz Shah Kotla Stadium in an hour. The practices have already started today," he finished and before I could think of any further clarifications to ask of him, the line was already dead.

I would have pinched myself to test the veracity of the situation, such was the disbelief. How did it come to this, I sat down and wondered. I don't get things so easily. Was this a joke? did someone play a prank on me? Muddled up in my thoughts and feeling maniacally happy at the same time, I was at a loss of expressions to let out these feelings. Once I collected my thoughts and reconciled with this fact, I heaved a sigh of relief. I undid the noose around my neck, symbolic of the slavery I was going to accede to and flung it to a remote corner of the room. I looked up and thanked God. All those trips to the Gurudwara finally bore their return on investment, the MBA in me figured.

I called up Hardik while changing into my gear simultaneously. It was a conversation filled with erratic sounds and a bundle of shouts. I let out all the happiness in that 3-minute call as I was already late for practice, rather induction, this time for the Delhi Daredevils and not the blood-sucking corporates, Holden Partners.

Just as I left, on my way to my bike, I called up Simi. The shriek let out by her, gave me a final confirmation of how much she cared for me, if there was any doubt about it in the first place. We decided to meet up in the evening, after practice. It was supposed to be my treat.

Besides myself with joy, I thumped along to the stadium. I made one final call to the HR at Holden, telling her that I had met with an accident and had fractured both my legs, while on my way to the doctor for my jaundice-related checkup. Hence, as ashamed as regretful I was, I had no other alternative but to cancel my internship, I told her.

The sweet lady she appeared to be, thanks to the perception I had garnered owing to the previous conversations with her, was actually a hoax. She was no less than a FBI agent and a pain in my posterior, asking countless questions about my health and my hospital whereabouts. At one point, I wanted to tell her the truth so that she could spare me the ignominy of further interrogation.

Finally, somehow I guess God intervened and she stopped. She told me to drop a formal mail declaring my withdrawal, when I was in the condition to do so. She also said that she regretted to inform me that Holden would not be able to give me an Internship completion certification. I agreed to all her terms and conditions and pitifully replied that I would somehow manage.

I didn't even want to think of the hell that would break loose in college when the placement team would come to know of the fast ones I had been pulling on such a coveted account like Holden. But frankly, at that moment, I couldn't care about anything or anyone.

I knew the protocol as I quickly changed into white overalls and rushed to the ground with my heartbeat crossing previously set limits, more out of incredulity of the events that had unfolded in the past hour than my sprinting dash to the ground. There were a few familiar faces, the ones from the elite 24.

I was on the lookout for the coach when my eyes noticed a Caucasian bloke, pudgy, semi-bald, possibly in his early forties and dressed in Slazenger track suit, the perfect stereotype of a coach. He had sharp black eyes, a perfectly carved face which his out of shape, body did not complement. The man would've been a ladies eye candy in his heydays, I figured. He sported a pair of snazzy sunglasses which were shoved up on this forehead.

"Sir, I am…" I was cut mid-sentence as I went up to talk to him.

"Vineet, right?" He spoke with an accent, obvious, but still noteworthy.

"Yes, Sir. I am here to replace... umm…the injured guy," I clarified.

"Yes, I know. Sandeep. The poor guy, had an accident, both legs fractured," he said with genuine sympathy showing on his face while shaking his head in a manner reeking of pity for Sandeep.

I chuckled at the coincidence, as if someone had heard my excuse and pasted it on the poor guy. Whatever! I thought; he anyways, did not deserve to be in this team. I never knew, Prakash and Pratap thought so highly of me, I thought joyfully. Finally, the struggle had borne fruit, the toil was worth it and the sour memories of the swollen body and aching legs now felt sweet.

"Warm up boy, and get to practice. Quickly do up ten rounds and then we'll start," said Mr.Coach, whose name I learnt was Nelson.

10 rounds! What on earth was the coach thinking?! I'm not a Kenyan marathon runner. If I run ten rounds, who will practice, my after life remains? I cussed the coach under my breath as I

started my rounds. I had heard these foreign coaches were hard nuts, but they were career finishers, I never knew.

Life was so simple with Sharma ji, I recalled.A gentle jog, a few stretches here and there and we were ready to roll, and here I was puffing, panting like a stray dog chased by someone whose food the poor one had tried to steal.

After I had lost half my body weight in the form of sweat, the ten rounds finally ended. Struggling to appear able enough to perform the physical chores the training demanded, I feigned an upset tummy. The coach, though a hard ass, appeared to buy this one.

I took permission to take medicine which was supposedly in my bag in the locker room which gave me an opportunity to catch some air.

I was going to be a member of the Delhi Daredevils and ten rounds sucked the air out of me. This was going to be exponentially tougher than I had ever constructed it to be. I reappeared on the ground a good ten minutes later.

Strolling aimlessly, trying to appear busy, I finally got a glimpse of the man I had idolised for a long time now. There he stood around five foot eight, partially bald with a small but noticeable protruding abdomen. He was having a dialogue with Nelson where he seemed to be discussing something related to the square cut. I wanted to run to him like a small puppy does to its mother with wide, expectant eyes, love dripping from them but I couldn't, after all I was his team mate. Eventually, unable to withhold the temptation, I went over once I saw he was alone and padding up.

"Hello, Sir."

"Call me Viru... and you are?" he said smiling.

"Sir, Vineet. I am a big fan of yours and it feels unreal to meet you," I spoke, against my wishes.

"I really admire your style of play,Sir." I said, as I noticed him from head to toe. The aura of the man was like that of any of us, normal, bare and if someone saw him on the road, he might not even command a second look. So ordinary, yet so extraordinary, I thought.

"Sir nahi yaar... Viru bolo," he corrected me again, though gently.

"Viru, I just wanted to meet you and tell you it is indeed an honour playing along side you," I completed, again sounding ridiculously servile, but I just couldn't help it.

"Don't be so formal Vineet. We'll have fun together, these 50-odd days!" he winked as he tested the three bats lined up in front of him, one after the other, finally zeroing in on the one looking the most menacing, before going in for practice.

Totally disregarding what I was there for, and observing the other members of my team who had sometime or the other represented the blue colours, I was like a boy on a beach, who was getting to see bikini clad women for the first time in his life.

" Hey Vineet, come here. Are you fine now or do you want a break for today?" said the coach, in his thick English accent.

"No sir, the meds have worked just fine. I am ready for the practices," I said, having partially recovered from that near-fatal jog.

Everything had happened so quickly that I failed to realise that the IPL commenced in a mere twenty days. The joy of being a part of the 30 had taken a backseat and now I knew that I had to try to vanquish a majority of these 30 to actually get to the playing eleven. Considering I was a waitlist, who had made this squad by a hair's breadth, it seemed an even more herculean task but I was never the one to give up, at least that's what I thought about myself.

"From what I know you are a batting all-rounder?" asked the coach.

"Yes sir. I like to believe that," I said solemnly.

"Pad up then." he said.

The drill continued the same way it used to in the selection camp. The quality of bowlers sure was notches higher but the monster training had done me a lot of good. As the days went by, which though were pretty uneventful, sans the fact that I got to see a lot of stars, I figured one thing that was the monster training had to be continued. If I had to be amongst the best, I had to compensate for all the years when I was studying how code gets compiled for a program.

Hence the same life-sapping routine began. After the training session, I would call up the two monsters, who were understandably reluctant to help me as they had no benefits of bowling like mad men to me all evening. A promise of beer and chicken every day after practice sealed the deal.

Gruelling practices continued through the week, with me mostly in the backdrop of the star-studded squad, when on a Friday, Viru came up with an idea, just an hour before the end of play. In an effort to bring some life into the otherwise mundane schedule, he suggested a small play.

Every batsman would face 25 deliveries and he'd try to dispatch as many to the boundary. Simple as it sounded, he made it simpler by declaring that there would be no fielders. To up the stakes, he announced the winner would be treated to a buffet dinner at the Taj Palace. A life that would have been brimming with visits to the Taj and the likes was what I had forgone to be there so it was not an offer to swoon over for me, but what impact it would make if I did something extraordinary in this perfunctory activity fancied by Mr. Viru, was what I weighed in my mind.

To top it, my forte was right here, to just hit the ball, as getting caught or being bowled were not threats anymore. Things don't get any more tailor made, I relished.

The newly-bought and much hyped Bowling Machine was set up. The coach volunteered for the ball- feeding job as the batsmen geared up. If there was a condition which exemplified nervousness and confidence at the same time, this was one such time. How important this trivial piece of play could be, I had already gauged.

There were twenty-four players in totality, a dozen of which were bowlers, which meant I was competing against twelve, including Viru. The six vacant slots were those of foreign superstars, who would make late appearances owing to a hectic international itinerary, though early entries into the final eleven were guaranteed once the IPL commenced.

There was no order and the players made random appearances. Nothing exceptional was witnessed in the first twelve odd plays, half of which were contested by bowlers or self-proclaimed all-rounders. Even the batsmen with the most exaggerated abilities could manage around 10 hits to the boundary.

Then was showcased the masterpiece, which effaced any minutest of doubts that he was a player who had been selected on the pure grounds of ability. Three, yes three hits to the boundary out of which two were outside edges and the third was the best French cut in the history of the game.

Vaibhav had made every person there fall to the ground, resigning to the hysterical laughter his antics had induced in them. Viru, usually the politest of them around, couldn't help but laugh like a small kid watching Vaibhav bat. Vaibhav, though, was a superb sport, and joined everyone by laughing his head off at the gag he had presented all of us with.

This waggery was followed by a series of decent performances with my favourite batsman in the team, apart from myself and Viru that is, Shashank, getting 16 boundaries. Nineteen team mates had gone by and Shashank held the record as of now, when entered yours truly.

With no past track record in the Ranji trophy, a name unheard of in the Delhi cricketing circles, and having created no ruffles during the selection either, I was an enigma for some and a formality for the others. From the looks of it, sometimes I got vibes that some guys here felt that even I was here on account of string pulling. Nevertheless, just like always, I offered a hurried mental prayer to God.

I never knew God took me this seriously too as I found myself on a rampage. I produced an unbelievable array of smashing shots, which even I didn't have cognition of, that I had them in my repertoire. It seemed as if there was a magnet at the centre of my bat and the ball kept hitting the G spot every single time, cranking out perfect strokeplay. A blinder of a knock later, twenty-one was my count, bettering Shashank's by a whopping 34%, I calculated, wondering simultaneously as to when this bug of mental calculations would leave me alone. I stood there, attracting glances from guys who hadn't even bothered to speak to me in these two weeks. It felt damn good.

The next two guys managed nothing miraculous either, with a thirteen and a ten, both of which were above par, but now looked ridiculous juxtaposed against the colossal figure I had set. Viru, the last one to come in, calm, unflustered by the looks of it, the one with nothing to lose, whilst bearing the weight of enormous expectation, though failing which would be inconsequential, had me now as a direct challenger. It wasn't easy to believe the events that had transpired in the last hour, with everyone in the background like mere spectators and the focus on the two of us.

Vineet Grover sharing the same pedestal as Virender Sehwag, with the odds stacked firmly against the latter and a high probability that this young twenty-three year old engineer MBA beat Viru at his own stronghold in his very own backyard.

Sporting a smile, I was praying harder than ever before to just let me have the glory this one time! It's funny how I managed to "this one time" God every single time, but I guess that's just me, trying to convince myself of not being a pathetic glutton.

Life repeats itself in cycles, that is, why the term déjà vu has been invented. I was always given the taste of victory, like a single 'Pringle' chip, but when it came to savouring the whole thing, God loved to see me grovel. Same old story, the story of my life, Viru smashed the monkeys out of the bowling machine, which by now appeared useless to me for the cost of a bloody million rupees. Deep down I also felt the coach, just to show us who was the daddy around there, must have eased the pace a tad. Unable to assimilate the absurd twenty-three boundaries Sehwag managed, the respect for him somehow grew manifold in my heart. The man indeed deserved his standing as the most destructive batsman on the face of earth. Even with divine intervention, I had failed to beat him.

There was a roaring applause and relief-filled sniggers, as the inevitable unfolded. The drama which could have taken a different direction now ended how it was expected to. Still managing a contrived smile, I was wondering whether to go congratulate Viru or not.The fact that my visage would give away my extreme displeasure owing to the drama that had unveiled, I held back.

Hesitant, frozen at the same place I had taken before he had started, I just couldn't understand what the right thing to do was, when the man himself walked up and acknowledged my effort.

"You really gave me a run for my money there. Anyways, superb hitting, man!"

"He's a guy to look out for, guys," he said as he winked again.

What was with the winks, I never fathomed, though his comment finally invoked a bright childish grin on my face.

"Though you didn't win the dinner treat at theTaj, but you surely deserve it," Sehwag said gleefully as I, at a loss of words, did nothing but smiled.

A black shining Mercedes which Viru claimed was one of his three vehicles, though without an iota of arrogance, was our ride to the hotel. Parking in the VIP Section and taking the VIP passage, I felt important though with a pinch of pity. What is life when one of the basic tenets of life, freedom, is at stake? That indeed was the price of being Virender Sehwag. However, all these thoughts vanished once I saw the buffet that was laid out. It would have at least taken a page to describe the buffet in its entirety, so I would let this one pass, only terming it as elaborate, a gross understatement for what was on offer.

Various matters were discussed, mostly involving cricket, leaving me dazed like a kid in a magic trick show. I did feel a little odd while asking him so many questions, but I shamelessly pursued this practice throughout the dinner, and the wonderful man that he was, he candidly answered all of them. By the end of the meal, I knew a lot more about Sehwag's favourite knocks, the sledging by the Australians included things that cannot even be discussed in a closed room, how Sachin was at a different pedestal than every other cricketer in the universe and how your internals felt like throwing up the whole time after getting hit by a 155 kmph delivery.

"Vineet, remember, play the way you know, that is how you got here in the first place. People will find 101 different flaws in you after every failure and the same flaws will become your uncanny knacks to score when you succeed. Bottomline, believe in yourself and the God above, and you shall go places," he spoke while on our way back and I swear I could see the halo above his head.

Saturday was a work day too, that is, by choice, when I chose to play Monster 1 and 2 again under the same mortal conditions gradually decreasing the length of the pitch till it was humanely impossible to touch the ball anymore. These bullets failed to hurt me anymore, the hits felt normal, like to a pugilist, who gets habituated to the blows across his skullnumb, unfeeling,accepting it as a part of who he is rather than what he aspires to be. Thanking them again with a Godfather beer and kake da chicken, I rushed home for a shower since I was to meet Simi in an hour.

Meetings and conversations with Simi had taken a new course. I had never imagined I would summon romantic feelings for her. But to be frank, it was only a question of how long I could not fall in love with her. I never said it, but it did become obvious to both of us, going by the exuberant unnecessary smiles between conversations, casual cuddly handholding and long pregnant pauses while out on meetings but still feeling comfortable just in each other's presence.

"I really like you Simi and this time it's not just as a friend," I said while sitting in her car, back from one of our dinners where we just sat looking at each other through the dim yellow of the lone flame that burnt while we comfortably ate our supper. Once I realised that I just couldn't control looking at her without not wanting to hug her tightly, wishing to never let her leave the confines of my arms, I gave in.

"I love you and no, this does not force you to say the same thing. These are my feelings for you and they've stayed the same irrespective of what you've felt for me." She said with a sparkle in her eye, invoking a gush of emotions in me.

I leaned over and kissed her which turned passionate and went on for quite some time until we saw two urchins standing by the side of the car, giggling. A little embarrassed, Simi drove away as we sat silently, content in the comfort of each other's presence.

"Won't you call me for coffee, you dumb ass?" she said, as I bid her adieu, while she dropped me home.

"Oh crap, I am sorry. Please come. I am a little too dazed after that kiss," I justified my clumsiness cutely. She came in and not a word was said when in a couple of minutes we were kissing fiercely.

It didn't take long before we found ourselves naked, lying atop each other making slow, rhythmic love, something that I had more or less predicted, when she mentioned coffee. It was slow and gentle, just like it was meant to be. It turned wild from time to time, may be perpetrated by the extreme physical attraction we shared for each other. She spent the night at my place as we slept cozily in each other's arms.

❖ ❖ ❖

CHAPTER 7

The Dream Lives –I

"Dream what you want to dream; go where you want to go;
be what you want to be, because you have only one life
and one chance to do all the things you want to do."

— *Anonymous*

The last couple of weeks before the IPL were pure crazy. Critics analysing unnecessary details, making useless predictions and the so-called strategy gurus of the game dishing out pathetic logical inferences to the team managers for decisions that baffled the brains out the of most.

Top it with contract-singing, brand endorsements, and silly inane ads sprawling everywhere which stretch their imagination to any extent to showcase their affinity towards cricket, one sure did get a portent that what was going to follow would be a nauseous, grandiose carnival of sorts, of something which is religion to a nation with the second-highest population in the world.

Suddenly, the foreign players and the cheer leaders were flying in; practices gave way to the "strategy meets" where the first few matches were won in rooms full of computers.

The feeling was surreal when I got my Delhi Daredevils gear. Maybe it was normal for the others who had represented their state some or the other time,but not for someone who was a cricket fanatic hardly a year back, and the only t-shirt he sported was with someone else's name inscribed on the back.

But there I was, not wearing a T-shirt which read Tendulkar 10, but Grover 07. I felt a little over awed as if asked to step in a pair of shoes I never thought would be mine, reminding me of the time my father had asked me to drive the scooter for the first time.

Engineer, to a software slogger, to a soulless MBA, to a passionate cricketer; it was a journey, the most important phase of which lay ahead. This one-year excursion sure had been mind-boggling.

IPL was a platform which catapulted youngsters to instant fame. No one cared about the triple centuries you'd scored toiling at the state level in the last decade, one innings of slam bang cricket and you made it to the selectors' list. The purists hated it, but sure as hell no one ever ignored it. Critics termed it as tamasha cricket, a mockery of the real game only to cater to the sensory pleasure of the spectator who wants to see the bowlers demolished, 50s and 100s scored in ridiculously low number of balls and if nothing else, then females in the skimpiest of attires shaking their booty to ugly hoicks which don't even deserve a clap. Boundaries were brought in, cheer leaders were set at every nook and cranny of the stadium and a DJ was set to up the ante when the cricketers failed to do so. It basically was like a party with a little cricket thrown in between.

But the bottom-line was that no one complained. The advertisers got their money's worth; the cricketers got paid insanely high even for the sometimes pathetic quality of cricket they produced, and the spectators got a three-hour more dramatic substitute for the sham-filled Bollywood movie.

The IPL commenced with much fanfare, the opening ceremony being the spectacle of a lifetime. The mere sight of the number of the people in the stadium set my pulse racing. Empty stadiums sans a few security guards was what I was used to and suddenly 40,000 eyes keenly watching me, apart from the many millions on TV, felt surreal. If stage fright was a term coined for debating in front of a hundred people at school, what on earth would this be called? It was indeed an over awing manifestation of the immense money that was being pumped into the biggest display of monetary clout, glamour, and India's favourite sport, all at the same venue.

❖ ❖ ❖

Our first match was lined up on the third day from the inaugural ceremony. The final team of twelve was going to be declared any moment, which induced a lot of undercurrents and rumours to circulate regarding the same. Expecting nothing much, as Delhi Daredevils was known for its powerhouse line-up, including four foreign players, stalwarts who'd already represented India and a couple of odd IPL/Delhi regulars, there was barely a slot for two new faces.

Being a waitlist from the selection camp, my chances were—to be fair—less than bleak. Apart from the "Good Friday" when I had flayed a bowling machine all over the park, I'd never got the opportunity to showcase my real skill and club cricket didn't count for much here. Hence, to be fair, I wouldn't have selected myself, had I been in the selector's shoes.How could I possibly expect them to?

It hurt a bit, as the foreseeable was announced. I did not make it to the first twelve for the first game. It was an away-game against Kolkata Knight Riders, the sorriest team in the history of IPL.

A tad gloomy, I was sitting by the swimming pool, after a rejuvenating session of swimming, lost in my thoughts sipping a Gatorade when Shashank approached me.

He was short but built like an ox, and observing his muscular frame, one could never imagine that he could run the twenty-two yards faster than anybody else in the team. Surprisingly his face was still childish,hence he liked sporting a stubble to negate the childish features. His eyes were dreamy blue and one would have imagined he'd be an advertiser's dream incase he makes it big in cricket.However, what one could make out was that when he'd hit the ball, it dare not fall inside the ropes for his hit was one of the fiercest, a fact to which everyone who'd seen him bat could swear by.

"So, what's up buddy? Didn't make it either eh?" said Shashank. He was one surprising omission from the list, the most prolific run scorer in the Ranji season, and someone who oozed talent if you saw him bat. We never really spoke, only exchanged obligatory pleasantries, but he was someone I liked both with regard to skill as a cricketer, and demeanour on and off the field.

"Yeah, but I wasn't even expecting it. But I seriously expected you to make it," I said candidly.

"I don't know man. I wish I had some contacts where it mattered. Like you," he winked as he said it.

"Yeah right. I wish!" I too laughed with him.

"No, seriously man. You are good, I saw you that day. Plus you have a decent pull with people that matter, it seems. I really thought you'd be there in the team," he spoke, now with a peculiar yet serious expression on his face.

"What do mean? I don't have any contacts." I explained, bewildered, losing the smile.

"It's nothing to hide man. Everyone uses contacts if they can. I like you and my advice to you is to use them to your best. Else you'll be sitting here, warming benches like me year after year." He spoke with frustration pretty visible in his sentence, leaving as he said it.

Baffled, I couldn't ingest one bit of what he had just said. What was he thinking, that this was a back door entry for me, I thought, visibly enraged.

"Oye listen, Shashank!!" I shouted. He turned around as I went running after him.

"I swear I didn't get one word of what you said. Could you please elaborate?" I asked, expectantly.

"Dude, it's none of my business, I didn't know that you didn't know that people knew. Sandeep, the guy you replaced, is a friend. He told me you're screwing Malhotra's daughter. I don't know whether you take me to be a complete imbecile or you yourself are one. Whatever it is, take care," he left again, this time with pace in his step clearly indicating he wanted no more of this.

Was he talking about Simi Malhotra? I felt a little dazed, unable to digest this fact. The puzzle of my selection that I had tried to solve and then shunned, by thinking that it must surely have been based on merit, was now unsolved again. Like a maze, the solution of which was not pointing towards any pretty conclusions, I shuddered at the thought of knowing the truth. The most celebrated achievement of my life was a farce, I gasped with disbelief. I immediately called up Simi.

"Hi baby. Was thinking about you only," I heard her cheerful sweet voice, after which it was usually difficult to say anything mean even if you wanted to. But that day was different.

"Who is you father, Simi?" I asked with a slight tremble in my voice.

"What kind of a question is that? What happened?" concern lurked over her two questions.

"Answer the question Simi,who is your father?" I asked again, this time more sternly demanding an answer at once.

"Ok!! I get it! My father is a 40% stake holder with Delhi Daredevils, that's what you have heard or wanted to know, isn't it?" she said with a tinge of sarcasm sprinkled generously across the frank statement she made.

"Yes and now go ahead and also tell me how my selection was a sham, a freakingback-door entry, and make me feel like the loser I really am," I spoke, almost seething with anger with a dark gloom around me in the otherwise superbly sunny hotel outdoors.

"It wasn't, yaar. Everyone uses a little contact. So what if I put in a word for you?Is it so wrong to do something for someone you love?" she said with her speech quivering and I could now sense that she would cry any moment now, propelling me to a guilt trip.

I disconnected the call, unable to listen to anymore of what had happened. How could I be so dumb not to have seen this the whole time? No prior Ranji record, no exceptional performances during the camp, players like me took years to find a place in the team and here I was, in the team the very first year itself. With what right did I want to be in the playing eleven when I wasn't even in the top thirty on merit? Shattered, with these thoughts internally tearing me apart, simultaneously trying to control myself from breaking down again, which was now beginning to become a routine, I flung my towel onto the nearest chair and jumped into the swimming pool again.

I swam till my arms were sore and unwilling to thrust me forward. I never knew whether I cried that day, having found the perfect camouflage in the pool, so perfect, even I didn't come to know when my tears, if they were there, became a part of the pool of self-pity and grief.

Seven missed calls, Simi had been trying to call me frantically. I called back.

"Yaar what is this, why weren't you taking my calls? I was worried god dam it!" she sounded desperately worried.

"Sorry. Was swimming.Had to find some place to let the steam out."

"What is your problem? What has happened that is so grave that you are behaving like this, Vineet?"

"It's just that the most cherished achievement of my bloody life is a joke, a farce. I never deserved to be here and trust me, it doesn't feel that bloody awesome."

"Ok. Tell me one thing. Do you agree you were better than many around there but still because no one knew you, hadn't seen you and because you didn't have any previous national career records, you never were considered for the selection seriously? Wasn't this what you've told me time and again?"

After the longest pause all I managed was a "Yes."

"So what the hell is wrong? All I did was believe in what you said, and as luck would have it, my father is a doting one and cannot say no to his daughter. And trust me; I can't do anything beyond this. Whatever headway you make now would be purely on the basis of your skill and talent. So if you make it big, good - and if you don't, we can consider you as a poor judge of yourself. Now stop whining Vineet, I know you'll make it big." She spoke quite convincingly, with shades of Hardik in her tirade.

Most of what she said was correct. How did the person who never passed one exam without peeking into the neighbours' copy become so self-righteous, I wondered?

"I love you, Simi," I mumbled meekly.

"And thanks for what you did...I'll not let you down." I spoke with wobbly conviction.

"I love you, too," she said as we ended the call over some small talk.

I reflected on what she had just said. Apart from admiring her "calming me" quality that she had recently acquired, she actually made perfect sense. I was cribbing all this time about not getting an opportunity to display my competence and hence suffering the brunt of non-selection and now that this God-sent angel had presented me with this perfect opportunity, I had snubbed her. Self-righteousness, my ass!The place was mine and I had got it, I thought as I chuckled to myself like a retard. Waiting for that one opportunity, biding my time, I thought of myself as a tiger in the dark, alone, patient, ready to pounce on the first opportunity that came within leaping distance. I slept to this thought which incited the worst nightmare featuring me in the body of a tiger coupled with my face. Not a pretty sight, I must say!

❖ ❖ ❖

Disaster struck. We lost to a team which was so lame, that all other teams had already added four points to their kitty for winning both their matches against them in the league stages, prior to the start of the tournament, that is. On a scale of 'lame, lamer, lamest,' they bordered on lamest and a new scale point lamestest, and we lost to them. Our supposed star-studded line-up had failed to post a decent score, heck, it was a disgraceful score of 112 which they made a shoddy work of. Winning by 6 wickets, the Kolkata Knight Riders had forced us to rethink our opinions about ourselves.

The match was followed by a frenzied meeting, right into the wee hours of the morning where the batsmen were caustically lambasted. Their careless approach was condemned and everyone was once again reminded of their role in the team. Not everyone was Batman, the Robins were reminded satirically. When you're meant to be the sidekick, behave like one, was the message loud and clear, in other words only a few had the license to go ballistic from ball one, others well, were Robins.

The two-day gap before the next match was supposed to be a breather. Practice was not what was concentrated on, team dynamics were. There was a lull around the whole time, courtesy the shock drubbing. None of the eleven had performed; hence a few from the eleven would get the axe, atleast that was what we were expecting.

When the same twelve names were announced later in the day whilst the team meet, it was a bit of a shock. But to be fair, though, the lads did deserve another chance, which was coming to them the next day against one of the goliaths of the IPL circuits, Chennai Super Kings, lead by the flamboyant Indian captain, MS Dhoni. The steep task that it appeared to be, the Daredevils themselves were no run-overs in this IPL format. Semi finalists in many a year, we were regarded as heavyweights, though our previous game's trouncing would have given a boost to every opponent.

I was fraught with mixed feelings about the results I wished from the next game. Whether I wanted the team to lose, resulting in major changes in the team composition or be a jingoist, putting the team's cause before self. Even though I knew that this wouldn't actually change the scheme of things, I still wanted to take a stance, hence it boiled down to me wanting the team to do well but only with the likes of the permanent members performing. A selfishly patriotic stance if there ever was one, was what I settled for.

The game against Chennai was again an away game at Chepauk. Watching the game from the dugout is the most frustrating thing one can do. Every time someone is screwing up in the middle, you feel like running out there and taking up the mantle yourself. I twitched, exclaimed, cringed and winced throughout the game as it was a close contest we watched, and finally lost.

First, the Super Kings made a mockery of our not-so-formidable bowling attack by posting 189 which was followed by a resolute and sublime batting display by our top four. At one time it appeared as if we would make it, but the inexperienced lot lost the chase in the middle overs and we ended up 12 runs short. Viru, despite his valiant 65, saw his team sink and just like mine, his helplessness was pretty palpable around the dugout. He sat alone in a corner wearing a frown of resignation on his face as the drama unfolded, and we lost a match we could have won.

Two out of two lost, for a team which counted amongst the favourites. There was some serious questioning the guys would be facing tonight, I thought, sensing that a change now was inevitable. How would I make it, was the question.

Third game would be too ambitious for me; I was expecting a chance somewhere around the seventh game of the season if we performed pathetically and if the performance was above par, then only once had we qualified for the semifinals, in the dead rubbers, that is. In both cases, many agony-filled frustrating days were left, I knew.

❖ ❖ ❖

Talking to Simi, I seldom showed dissent or expressed my extreme desire to play that elusive first game. I suppressed it, trying to always divert the topic if it ever cropped up. It led to a lot of frivolity during our conversations, but anything to have my ego blasted again. She would time and again goad me to tell her what exactly was going on, but I would just put her off by some impromptu clever smart-ass statement and convince her that my first game was not very far, whereas in reality I knew this was something that might not even happen.

After all, a man's ego and pride were sometimes the sole entities he has to live on. Additionally, I would be confident being a part of the team only if I made it to the team on merit. Else the hollowness of the back-door selection would forever be gnawing at my insides, I figured. I would ensure it by subtly slipping it in our conversations, that if she tried to help me again, it would break me as a cricketer and as a person and maybe I would never be able to look her in the eye again. I knew she cared too much for me to kill my pride.

❖ ❖ ❖

The team meeting before the third match was a little calmer as compared to the last one. Naturally our performance had bettered, just that we lacked the knockout punch, claimed the coach. Expectantly sitting, everyone was waiting for the team announcement. I, though, was not expecting a call and I had made a mental waitlist, from which I was praying for the first few to move the queue.

Shashank and, wait for it, the jackass Vaibhav were going to get a look in for the next match. There are seldom so many emotions in a single room at the same time;from disappointment to awe, to disbelief, to exultation (only Vaibhav), to wry smiles (the men from the CEO's office), to utter disgust (Viru and co.). The room suddenly filled with hushed whispers and majority of the occupants were now giggling at the most pathetic joke that had been cracked in a lifetime. No one knew whose contacts Vaibhav used, but from the looks of it, they couldn't have been any ran lower than the president of the BCCI.

The whole evening there were private room meetings and the stunned silence was literally palpable.

The next day we faced off against the Rajasthan Royals, a team known for its mercurial performances. One day they will play like champions and the next just crash like a house of cards. Led by the master Shane Warne, no one ever took this, otherwise weak team, lightly.

For the first time in cricket, it must have been a ten on eleven game. Viru made sure to make his objection, evident in every decision he took. Not a single over was given to Vaibhav, heck it became so evident that we thought he would declare not to let Vaibhav bat even if we were nine down. For once, I felt bad for Vaibhav, a neat-looking guy, his hair combed as if his mummy just did it, only communicating via smiles or frowns, he remained to himself. The answer to the suspense as to who backed him was something desperately sought by every team member.

Batting first, we had piled up a 168, a reasonable total by T20 standards and even with a bowling handicap in Vaibhav, it was defendable, we'd known. Defend well we did, but only till the eighteenth over when thirty runs were required of the last two overs and need I mention, they were given away. With specialist bowlers done with their quota coupled with the fact that Vaibhav wasn't getting one, the ball had to be tossed to the part-timers, who could not be blamed as the Royals' fiercest strikers were on the crease.

With uncomfortable questions cast towards Viru in the post-match conference about the 'curious case of Vaibhav' we knew the issue had hit the roof. What would follow would either be a complete media- induced outcry about the politics involved in IPL or a quest for complete control by the players and the coach and no management intervention henceforth.

A livid Viru sat in the bus with his eyes closed, and understandably no one sat on any seat within a one meters radius of him. A volcano waiting to erupt and my team losing every match it played, not the very particular start one wants from his career.

"Hey there!" I shouted as I saw Shashank the next day.

"What's up, man?" he asked.

"All good all good, by the way you played well yesterday," I complimented him on his 38 off 21 balls.

"What's the point? We lost anyway," he sounded dejected as he stood there in his shorts exposing the most muscular legs I had ever witnessed in person.

"I know man, but we were ten against twelve and their twelve included the star of the match,Vaibhav," I chortled, turning my sight away from his legs, only to notice his ripping arms that were almost about to tear out of his T-shirt.

"Yeah man, poor guy though. By the way who the hell is he?A couple of club matches and straight to Delhi Daredevils?"He inquired, unintentionally pinching me where it hurt.

"Don't take it the wrong way, for me you are a pretty good player even though you share a certain similarity with Vaibhav in terms of cricket history but that guy is a mind-numbing retard, man," he added quickly, noticing my silence.

"Yeah it's ok, people are bound to feel a little awkward when lads without busting their asses off on the domestic circuit straightaway make it to this level. And I have no clue who that Vaibav's Godfather is," I claimed.

"Hmm. What else, you ready for an entry into the next match?" he said laughing.

"Don't joke yaar, you know I'm not making it to the eleven so soon, if at all!" I spoke with a pinch of resignation in my tone.

"Oh you shall see, I know Viru has a thing for you," he chuckled.

"Screw you man!" I said, as we shared a laugh.

I ran straight to the Gurudwara, first thing after my name was announced at the meeting. I had replaced Vaibhav. Vineet Grover - this name had never sounded as awe-inspiring as it did that day. Once the name had been called, the multitude of eyes that shot me glances said it all, what it really meant. Admiration, envy, and maybe congratulatory looks filled up the room. I have never tried so hard to repress emotions, for which 'strong' would be a rank understatement. I had this pleasure-wave oscillating from my spine to my brain.Surreal as it was,the dream of a lifetime had seen its first bit come true.

I shrieked like a little boy who had just seen a ghost, while on call with Simi. She also went ballistic with her 'I love you' and 'I am proud of you' and all I could gather was a flurry of uncontrollable silly sounds which made no sense. I had to take heavy breaths once in a while, gather my thoughts and convince myself that it had really happened.

The call to Hardik was just the same as always, filled with profanities and promises of parties that would have scantily-dressed women and alcohol in quantities unheard of. It came to levels where the word exaggeration was redefined.

There was an immense instinct to open up a bottle of chilled beer and celebrate the occasion with Simi, but I had to commit myself as a responsible individual as this opportunity was not one to be squandered.

Congratulatory pats and handshakes took up the evening. Same as on the day of the CAT, I couldn't down a single morsel of food for the rest of the evening. I sipped on a solitary can of juice as I entered my room at ten after watching a movie with a few team mates. I couldn't recall one single sequence of the movie, as my mind was anticipating the probable future that lay ahead. I lied down knowing it would be a long, sleepless night. I could see the street-lamp from my hotel window. I observed as cars zoomed past on the highway that reflected the mild moonlight. With my eyes transfixed on the road, my mind frenzied through the gamut of possibilities that awaited me the next day. I closed my eyes a few times trying to sleep, but that wasn't happening. Finally, when dawn broke and Delhi welcomed a cool, clear morning, somewhat entangled in my thoughts, I finally found sleep. A mere three hours later, the 8 a.m. alarm made the cell phone beep it's batteries out, and I sprung up knowing that it was time to gear up for the day of my life.

A filled-to-its-capacity Feroz Shah Kotla Stadium is a spectacle in itself. Surely a small country could completely fit into the stadium with still some vacant seats. Extending up to three tiers, it felt like a Roman coliseum. The chants of people coupled with the intimidating size of this gigantic structure could make you knot in your stomach, just by the thought of standing in the middle and trying to play.

The encounter was with the Bangalore Royal Challengers, a mediocre team, definitely lower seeded than the Daredevils, but with the form we were in, even the 'Bangalore Physically Challenge ders' could have beaten us. With a good mix of youth and experience, their team had bettered since the last few seasons and the critics expected a lot from them this time round.

"We've already lost three matches, guys. We have to win a lot from here if we want the semi-finals spot. You are a talented bunch and trust me - we can and we are going to kick some Bangalorean ass today!" said Viru, trying to inspire and instill confidence in a burnt-out lot, but with a laid-back guy like Viru, it's tough to get inspired by his spoken word, though when the man brandishes his bat, it is a different story altogether.

We won the toss and chose to bat. The noise in the ground was deafening by the time. Viru and Gautam, our other swash buckling opener, walked in. If Viru had the killer instinct, this guy brought in calm into the camp. His composure reflected both in his style of play and his polite demeanour in the camp.

The atmosphere in the stadium, as some of the lame commentators would put it, was indeed electrifying. I was sitting there sweating, in a dilemma as to what I should actually ask for. Should I get to bat today or would we win without my contribution? The latter was the safer option but the former was the one which could either make me or break me.

Jumbled up in these thoughts and used to the incessant clamour by now, I was jolted out of my reverie by complete silence. Viru's off-stump had been rattled a few feet back by Mr. Dale Steyn. The hushed silence was the result of Viru's walk back to the dugout. Dilshan, our man from Sri Lanka, made his way in.

The tempo again picked up from where Viru left off and it was all going well till, in his second spell, Steyn obliterated our entire top order. From a position of reasonable comfort of 121/2, we slumped to one of uncertainty at 136/5. With five overs remaining, I stepped in. The moment I set foot inside the boundary ropes, I heard them announce my name, and it echoed all around the stadium. Extreme joy intermingled with butterflies in my stomach overpowered me. The crowd welcomed me with a mild cheer, though loud enough to give me goosebumps.

I tried hard not to be overwhelmed and to concentrate on the situation, understanding the fact that I was the senior batsman now with respect to skill, as I had a bowling all-rounder, Vinesh, at the other end.

"40 in four should be our target," he said, as I checked the pitch more out of formality and convention rather than intending to find anything worthwhile on it.

"No. Let's play by the over and set targets, else we'll mess it up," I suggested to a five-year Ranji-playing veteran. After eyeing me with suspicion and discovering deep-rooted conviction in my eyes, he nodded in agreement.

He stole a single in the first ball and gave me the strike. I immediately wanted to go and shake hands with Jacques Kallis, one of my many childhood heroes, but as of now he was an opponent, whom I had to treat with disdain, not by my mannerisms but by my batting display. I wish I had the words to describe how it felt when he came in running to deliver the ball. Before I could have witnessed the so-called flashes of my life in its entirety as a short 5-second film and see how all of it had culminated to this day, I had to be ready to take strike.

For a 36-year old man, he was admirably quick. I poked tentatively at a perfect delivery outside the off-stump. '87 mph' - the speed gun claimed. Not a very good ball to face the first time in your professional career. Phew!I knew instincts had to take over and caring about the consequences was only going to make me look like an idiot as has been the case the previous delivery. I still remember the next two deliveries as those were the ones I had smashed so hard that the reverberations from the bat, when the ball hit the not-so-sweet spots, had sent a hum down my spine. One was smashed through the covers bisecting the fielders, as if done using the perpendicular bisector theorem, and the next one over mid-on, like a perfect Diwali rocket cracker. I was pounding Jacques Kallis, forgive me cricket Gods, it's a part of my job description, I defended myself in my mind.

The Indian legend, Anil Kumble, was up for the next over. Tall, graceful like a puma on the prowl and a fighter to the core,he let out what was a ripper to Vinesh and saved him the agony of facing more of Kumble. Inept enough not to understand even a single delivery of that over, I managed to get only a solitary outside-edge to the boundary. The ball didn't spin at all but he was an enigma, like he has been for almost two decades now, for batsmen around the globe. I didn't know why I couldn't, let alone play, even touch Mr. Kumble.

Then came what I'd always dreaded the most in my life - extreme raw pace. Steyn had already tasted blood that day, no less than three times, and I knew he'd be spewing venom in this over, too. Uncertain about what he was planning on doing to me and remembering what mortal damage the two monsters had inflicted on me using a mere rubber ball, I checked whether every piece of padding on my body was there where it should've been, though in a subtle manner.

Full, straight and bloody fast;the red cherry misses the bat by a good light-year. Leg stump flies four feet back. Hushed silence. No-ball called. Feroz Shah Kotla erupts. Heart had missed six beats in a row. Yes, this indeed was the exact chronology of events that transpired in that span of five-odd seconds. I had been conferred a second life by some holy spirit lingering on the ground, that I was sure of. The speed gun showed 96 mph. SHIT!. Even if I had instructed the monsters to bowl balls at me from a one-arm distance, it couldn't be this fast.

Free hit and a license to swing like a madman, I thought.

But what I also knew was if the last one was fast, this one would be faster, not that there was a lot of scope left in that department. What would only vary was the length and so it did. Short pitched, sharp and rising like a tsunami which I knew would kill me, but any evasive action to duck or sway away would also fall short, that also I was acquainted with. With no other option at my disposal, I swung my bat like a fly-swatting bored housewife, with my eyes looking exactly 180 degrees away from the ball, what cricket basics I say. I knew I had hit the ball, but where, I had no clue. What I heard was the most deafening roar of my life. The ball flew and flew and then flew some more into the stands for the biggest six I'd hit in my life. One minute you're trying to save your brains from being blown out and the very next, you are making the crowd go wild.

Steyn ran up to me, gave me the eye and then mouthed something, none of which I could comprehend. It did, however, include generous use of the words 'mother' and 'f***.' I wanted to give some back to him, but with him in that mood and with that pace at his disposal, I thought better of the situation.

What happened next was the perfect reply, better than any mother-sister-father insulting abuse I could have managed. Planting my front foot forward without even seeing where the ball was pitched, which it thankfully did where I wanted it to, I belted the full-length delivery right over his head for another six. If the last roar was deafening,the roar that followed, I am sure, could have been heard in the neighbouring states.

Boy!Try hitting a pace bowler for one six and he's ready to rip your throat out Mortal Kombat style.I just doubled the humiliation and his aggravation.

A new lad, never heard of, twenty-three years of age, doing this to the world's fastest bowler, twice, was adding insult to injury. On the seventh heaven by now, my t-shirt felt tight against my pumped-up chest. I took guard to what I now knew would be a toe-crushing yorker or a head-bludgeoning bouncer, the two nuclear weapons of a pace bowler. I discounted the fact that fast bowlers also have brains, which was proven by the classic slower ball he managed to deliver.

It doesn't help when you're expecting something at 92 mph and it gets delivered at a 75 mph. Till the brain caught and assimilated this jarring gap, I had committed to a full-blooded swing. The result was an easy LBW after a manic appeal by Steyn. He ran past me this time, telling me to screw myself, though in a more uncouth manner. A little dejected, I knew though, that I had played my part. Looking at the giant screen I saw the 27(12), indicating the 27 runs I had scored at a strike rate of almost 225. Not anything that would set the stands on fire but a cameo, just enough to get me noticed. I walked back shaking my head, more as a ritual than as an expression of feelings that brewed inside me. Pats on the back awaited me since I had rescued my team from a precarious position. I was the second-highest scorer for my team right after my South African team mate AB de Villier's sensible knock of 51. Eventually, we managed to post a formidable total of a 186, thanks to the heroics in the last overs by the tail-enders.

The challengers started briskly though steadily without losing any wickets in the first few overs. Fielding at third man, I kept looking at Viru with my peripheral vision, after every over, waiting for him to give me the "start warming up" signal,usually given by doing circular motions with your arms. The signal finally came after the tenth over when they were at a better-than-decent 90/2 with two well- set batsmen at the crease.

The first few deliveries were right on the money. I was constantly eyeing to slip in a yorker, when it went horribly wrong and ended up as a full toss which was obliterated by Kevin, deposited way into the second tier of the stadium. Welcome to the big boy league, I thought. Very cautiously having measured me, he gave me the treatment right after two deliveries. I didn't experiment any further and bowled the conventional good length to restrict the over to 9 runs somehow.

Bangalore was cruising at 131/2 after 14 overs and Viru, as it was characteristic of him when edgy, had already started biting his nails. A little tension had started seeping in and we needed wickets desperately when I went in to bowl my second over.

Bowling at a lively pace of around 84 mph, I dug in the first one short, into the batsman's ribs. Unable to fend the ball, it hit him flush into the rib cage. He lay down, gasping for air and writhing in pain. I went up and apologised, but I guess the boy had cracked a rib. I felt sorry for him but at the same time, I was a little thrilled as I had broken the partnership, albeit unconventionally. The poor fellow trudged away to the medic van.

In came Ross, one of the most dangerous finishers in the game. In the meantime, I kept oscillating between reality and fantasy where I wondered that even if I had played for India, I wouldn't have played against so many mavericks in a single day; Kallis, Kumble, Steyn, Pieterson, Boucher and now Taylor. What a list!I gasped.

"We'll bounce him twice and then slow-ball him… ok?" said Viru, running up to me, having already placed a deep third man for the pull.

"But he's an exceptional puller,Viru bhai," I said, taken aback at these stupid tactics, as they appeared to me.

"It's his first ball. Just do as I say," he said in a convincing, though authoritative tone, something a newbox dare not disobey.

What the hell!I thought. I bowled the next one with all my strength, and the instinctive puller that he is, he pulled the delivery right in front of square leg for a crushing boundary. I glanced at Viru straightaway, he glanced back, and gave me the 'trust me' look. Back to my run-up, mentally abusing Viru for getting me screwed, I confirmed again about the short delivery. He returned the confirmation.

It was short and he went for the pull again, though this time he was going for a six. The ball went up miles in the air. Frozen there in my run-up, uttering God's name at a rapid pace, I saw Sandeep with his eyes fixed on the ball and back-peddling to the boundary. The ball was still sailing. No God, not a six!, I almost begged. It then appeared as if God, upon hearing my last imploring cry, bequeathed Sandeep with superpowers, thanks to which he flung himself towards his right side, with his right hand outstretched as far as possible, and plucked the ball out of thin air. The stadium erupted and the emcee went ballistic. Maybe I am biased, but I still feel it was, by far, the most stupendous catch I had ever seen in person.

Pumped up, I was now belting out bullets. It was the last ball of my over and I decided to go in for the good old yorker again. Yorker it was and a great one at that , with the ball banana-swinging like a kick from a Brazilian footballer and crashing straight into Mark's leg stump. He stood there gaping, not wanting to leave the crease, still unsure that what he had seen was real. Balls swing like that only in EASports Cricket computer games or when bowled byPakistani fast bowlers, and I was neither. Even Waqar Younis would have been proud of that one. I had never reverse-swung a ball before, but today out of nowhere, came out one extraordinary delivery -three batsmen accounted for in one over. Talk about dream debuts! I walked back to my corner to some really lively cheering by that section of the crowd.

At 138/4 and effectively 5, scoring at 10 an over was a herculean task and so it proved to be. They fell short by a good

20 runs and there it was - the first victory for the Daredevils, scripted majorly by Vineet Grover.

The night was filled with hundreds of calls and messages. Half of them were on the lines of "Dude, was it really you?" I got so tired of answering them that I had to switch off my phone for the day. Facebook was flooded too; all the long-lost friends had identified and then located me on Facebook. I just wished the HR at Holden wouldn't have seen the match, but then even if she had, she'd understand, I wishfully thought.

I switched on the phone later that night to talk to Simi and Hardik, the two integral cogs of the system that lead me to where I was today. I had made it to the team on my merit and had performed against men of repute and had proven myself. I felt confident like never before, even if it was just this one time.

❖ ❖ ❖

"You did well, Vineet," said Viru, as a few of us had dinner together.

"You really screwed Steyn, man, and fast bowlers loathe that!" Mr. 135 said, sniggering.

"Yes!and that hell of a yorker -what, did you programme that ball?" asked de Villiers with smiling disbelief.

"It was a good day is all I can say," I smiled, content with my accomplishments for the day, and still unable to believe that all that had actually happened.

The practice sessions now seemed better. There was more attention showered upon me, both by the coach and people who mattered, as I was now an integral member of this formation, I guessed. I was doing more bowling practice as they wanted me to change my batting all-rounder tag to more of a genuine all-rounder. More hours of practice were put in than ever before. Usually not a very wise thing to do, I asked Mr. 135 to give me short ball practice till I actually felt comfortable with the ball rising to dangerous heights. I slowly but surely honed each aspect of my game, trying to fill in any deficiencies by stop gap measures, at least for the time being.

❖ ❖ ❖

CHAPTER 8

The Dream Lives–II

"He who fears being conquered is sure of defeat."

— Napoleon Bonaparte

It was a welcome three-day break for the team before the next encounter, but somehow, for me, there were only tense, sleepless nights. I mostly plotted about how I was going to shape my career from there on. Mentally batting out the next match, facing lethal bowlers, hitting sixes, acknowledging the crowd after the standing ovation they confer me with for the sparkling hundred I've just treated them to, was mostly how my nights were spent. Lost in the congregation of these thoughts, I was usually too delirious to get any sleep. When I finally did manage to get some sleep, mental pictures of me losing the plot to fiery fast deliveries gave me recurrent goose bumps.

Punjab Kings Eleven was the team we faced off with, in the next game. A team marred by mediocrity both in terms of Indian players and players from the foreign contingent, with the exception of Yuvraj and a couple of others, they were not really a team that would send shivers down your spine or give you disturbed nights.

Comprising of one of the shoddiest bowling line ups in the IPL,they sure were rated along with the Kolkata Knight Riders in terms of their ability to get their ass whipped easily.

It was again a home game at the pantheon of cricket in India, Feroz Shah Kotla (many believe it is the Eden Gardens, but just taking into account the sheer number of India cap-bearers this ground produces, I award this revered position to Feroz Shah Kotla) and we enjoyed home advantage for that game, which already promised to be a one-sided affair, given our recent form. To top it, they were already struggling in this edition of the IPL, having won only one of their four games and unsurprisingly, the team they thrashed was Kolkata.

Expecting a somewhat early start to bowling in this match,, my belief came true when I came in to bowl inside the powerplay with Yuvraj in at 13/2. Talk about counter attack! He plundered me to all parts of the ground in that one horror-filled over. 4 4 0 4 6 0 read the giant screen. What had I done!I cursed myself. Couldn't I have bowled a bouncer, or a yorker? Why did the best fielder in our side misfield during one of my deliveries? So many questions -no answers! The worst had happened and like with all bad things, this wasn't coming back either. This would only transform into a phantom pain that haunts for times to come, I was sure about that.

Now all I could do was curse, both myself and Yuvraj, standing at my position at third man. I knew there would be no more bowling for the day, or maybe even the next match. Not only had I leaked runs like the way a creaky roof in a slum leaks water in the monsoons, I had helped Punjab, and more importantly, helped 'Yuvraj' gain momentum, which was a cardinal sin. From the last match's crowd darling, I had turned into a villain, and my section of the crowd imparted me the choicest of Hindi abuses at the boundary line as a reward for that. I had this intense want to show them the finger, but I held on to my nerve, still aghast at the beating of a lifetime I had just suffered.

Despite my anti-heroics, our bowlers pulled the game back and as expected, I never got another over. We kept them to 139, rather I should say that I tried to take them to a 180 but the other bowlers kept them to a 139.

It wasn't a very thrilling game as we crushed them with all our might, the crowd going inordinately crazy by the blitzkrieg run chase by Viru and the other top-order batsman. With a twenty required of five overs, it was a mere formality to be completed. That was the time I walked in to the crease to join Viru, the score solid at 120/4. I was instructed to play steadily as no more risk-taking was necessary for this cake walk, but I had other plans in mind. What better than to impress the captain by a little brisk innings to seal the victory in style?I thought. The mediocre bowling attack had only facilitated this thought process.

A part-timer came to roll his arm and identifying it as the perfect moment to seize the advantage, I launched his very first delivery into orbit. A fielder was waiting to humiliate me further, at the ropes. He took a not-so-simple catch, as the ball tends to gets lost in the lights at such moments, though that day it didn't. Why would it have?It was a day to get messed up, and messed up is what I got. What I also got was one of the coldest stares from Viru as I momentarily exchanged looks with him while walking the long walk of shame. It wasn't the shot selection, but the order-defying stunt I had pulled off that amounted to blasphemy.

Shit, Shit, Shit, I babbled, kicking myself, after wasting an opportunity to mildly redeem myself from the shameful excuse for an over I had delivered earlier in the day.

We won the match easily at the end, but I could not ingest the desecration I had committed on the field that day. My bowling had been decimated, and all the confidence accumulated in the previous game had been shoved down the drain. To top it off, I had enraged the captain, by whose goodwill I was there in the first place, playing for Delhi. In a moment of utter idiocy I blew it, just like that. Sudden pangs of wanting to bang my head on every sturdy thing in sight kept bugging me. So irritated was I, that I unnecessarily fought with Simi on the phone.

Realising my mistake, I sent a flowery message describing her beauty and my feelings for her, using the longest excerpts comprising of abstruse English words and all my poetic creativity, but to no avail. In no better mood, I let it go, letting the best healer take care of this one—time.

The sleepless nights had now started bugging me as for some reason or the other, I never could sleep peacefully. Tossing about, shedding one cloth after another, citing physical discomfort as a reason for my misery, I came to a point where I lied down with nothing but an irritated mind on me. I gradually realised the reason for this insomnia was something else. Nervousness about my future as a cricketer, now combined with a predicament I myself had created, put me in this insomniac position. Unrest was slowly decaying me; the need to do well at what I was passionate about, had become extremely overwhelming. I couldn't sleep during success; I couldn't sleep during failure. What was becoming of me?, I wondered.

There wasn't much time to rethink and restrategise as the next game was only a day away. I was befuddled about what my approach should be for the next game as it had become extremely important to perform to remain a part of the team. The day arrived while I spent another night battling the demons of chronic sleeplessness. After the morning breakfast, on a casual stroll, Viru came and chatted up.

"Hey, how are you?" he asked.

"I am good. Wanted to apologise for that day, but couldn't summon up enough courage."

"Oh, don't be silly. It's sport. Things like these happen a lot and don't take anything I say to you on the field to heart. In the heat of the moment, the situation gets the better of us. You'll see that with time."

"That's ok, Viru. I look up to you." I said the truth though this sentence surely might have fallen under the servile talk category.

"Oh no, don't look up to me. Ask the critics, they'll tell you what an impatient impulsive idiot I am," he smirked.

"Oh the critics even criticise Sachin, they aren't even worthy of being discussed," I reasoned.

"Yeah I know. Anyways don't take too much pressure, you seem to have not slept too well, your eyes are all red and stuff," he said.

"Oh no! I slept all right. I shall try and perform my best today."

"I am sure you will. Best of luck! See you in the bus," he said as he left.

The exchange made me feel a little better somehow. Maybe I wasn't as pathetic as I thought myself to be. I felt rejuvenated, thanks to the conversation,and I went up to my room for the last-minute preparations.

❖ ❖ ❖

Vijay Merchant, Sachin Tendulkar, Sunil Gavaskar graced the stands at the Wankhede Stadium, while I stood in the centre doing the final round of warm-up and practices. Every ground has a history, a history so strong as it can enamour you to the core. Speaking to the people around there who narrate incidents about the great legends of the yesteryear, we got to know how they had spent their years toiling and sweating and how it all summed up and made them who they were. Such inspiring anecdotes established a special bond that I shared with that stadium and deep down inside, lit a strong desire to leave an indelible mark at that hallowed venue.

Mumbai Indians at their home ground were virtually unbeatable, a statement which drew strength from their record in the last two editions of the IPL. Two evenly-matched sides with the exception of the fact that one side had 'God' in it. Sachin Ramesh Tendulkar, I could write a whole chapter on him, 'raving, ranting, praising,' and still fall miserably short in describing even half the man he actually is. A few lines that for me have described the man are:

"Beneath the helmet, under that unruly curly hair, inside the cranium, there is something we don't know, something beyond scientific measure. Something that allows him to soar, to roam a territory of sport that...forget us, even those who are gifted enough to play alongside him cannot even fathom. When he goes out to bat, people switch on their television sets and switch off their lives."

These lines were mouthed by some erudite-looking gentleman on BBC sports sometime in the nineties and these lines have been memorised and repeated and then repeated some more by me, to friends, relatives, family and anyone with whom I strike up a conversation on cricket.

It was a bright day, dry, something unusual for Mumbai as we bowled first, again. If I could, I would have frozen the moment in time, that was about to come, and store it for an eternity. In came God, five foot six, the only man even a Delhi Daredevil fan would like to see play well. An ordinary start be jeweled with some extraordinary strokes by the great man kept them at 36/0 after six overs.

To my surprise, the skipper called me on to bowl early, even after the last match drubbing I had suffered. His exhibiting confidence in me gave me a little self-assurance.

That was thc moment of my life and I could say pretty confidently, that never would a moment come again that could be more exhilarating than this one. Something that would even be above the 'placed at Holden Inc.'point on my resume. As taught in my MBA classes, the most important points of your text are stated using bullet points, hence, here I go:

- I have bowled to Sachin Tendulkar.
- He had found me worthy enough to defend my first delivery.
- Hc found me worthy enough to duck under my next delivery which happened to be a bouncer, intending no harm to the God I worship.

- He found me worthy enough to dispatch my next two deliveries to the boundary, to two of the most sublime cover drives, none better than the other.
- And, finally, he found me worthy enough to show me in full flow what the best of the forward defences looked like, in the final two deliveries. The surreal sequence concluded as I jogged back to my position, still emotionally overwhelmed by what had just chanced upon me.

They played along nicely and Sachin kept showing us why even at 37, he was still feared, as he stood there compiling a pristine fifty. I bowled two more expensive overs and went wicketless in the game while they put up an unnerving 167 on the board.

With Mumbai having an all-star bowling line up, we knew we were up against it, just that we couldn't let the tension be palpable, hence the coach and Viru spoke a few inspiring words during the fifteen-minute break, citing the target as a meager one and touting the pitch as a batsman's paradise though everyone knew neither of the two was true.

Seven overs into our batting, and we were in a mess at 42/3.Things looked extremely bleak, when I was thrust up the order. "Play your game," said Viru when I walked in, determined to make it my day. Inspired by the God, after having seen him from close quarters, I wanted to pull my team out of this rut.

Three balls into my innings, I smashed Malinga down the ground for a four. It's always great to get your first runs in the form of a boundary and if the manner is as swash buckling as this, the confidence absolutely surges.

The next ball was as pacy, with more steep bounce to which I offered a slashing blade towards backward point, but the Gods be damned, all I managed was a thick outside edge to the first slip that was just placed there, a ball prior to that one and that was the end of that. Stunned at my sheer stupidity, I wanted to ask for one more chance like we did when we were small kids. But for events broadcasted on national television, such outlandish requests are apparently not accepted. I walked back to the dugout like a woman, probably seven months into her pregnancy, cursing the Gods and myself with equal fury. I was carefully wrecking my career with every match, bowling like a jackass and then batting like a bigger one. I phased out for the rest of the game, jerking back intermittently at every wicket or six hit. The former was a much frequent event than the latter as we bundled up to a lowly 98 and to be truthful, it was more of an embarrassment than a defeat.

I sat at the last seat alone, wondering, hating the erratic path my career was following. A decent start and then two miserable outings -was I actually not good enough?I ruminated. This is not how frequently good players fail; first with the ball, then the bat, then again the cycle getting repeated!

With my reasoning skills completely squashed by my on-field antics, I felt may be Simi had again put in the word for me and that was why Viru had tossed me dirty looks in the morning. I could now fathom why his talk had hints of sarcasm and I was a dolt enough not to comprehend it. There was no reason for me to be picked ahead of so many other players with proven past records, and thanks to her again, it had been proven I was no good at this level. As this thought process became more persuasive, I saw myself literally boiling with anger.

As the bus halted, I scurried to my room to speak with Simi.

"Hi baby."

"Why did you do it again, Simi? Hadn't I asked you not to? Now look at me, the fool I've made of myself. I honestly hate you." I scowled.

"What are you even talking about? What did I do?" she feigned innocence, I gathered.

"Don't lie again, please, for heaven's sake. I had told you not to push my name again, I know your dad is a big shot, please don't rub that fact again and again and crush my pride with it." I was whimpering by now.

"Seriously, Vineet, I haven't said a thing. Believe me, I didn't. I had promised you I wouldn't and I didn't. Trust me!" she sounded too genuine to lie.

"Not this time. Thanks for the first time but I told you not again. I told you. I fucking told you, godamm it!" I had broken down by now, sobbing like a child and blaming her for the push she had apparently given me.

Not able to withstand the pain of failing my passion, I felt the writing was on the wall. The decision of giving up everything for the pursuit of this distant dream was horribly wrong. Of course, lads don't walk into this game and become pros overnight. All those heroes and mavens I have wished to emulate have put in countless hours of their lives into this sport, keeping everything else as a sub-priority. They are not from MBA colleges, with makeshift batting techniques developed against rubber balls and girlfriends whose fathers have enough clout to set them up in a team. They have risen from mines, like uncut diamonds, who have polished themselves year over year, sacrificing the luxuries of a customary life, chasing an illusion which seldom turns into reality, having seen uncountable episodes of failures amongst contemporaries, still perseverant enough to continue and endure, in a quest to see that light blue cap on their head and a jersey which reads India at the back. I am nowhere close to this, and why am I even expecting any such miracle? I thought pensively as I lay there in a melancholy mood, with the lower periphery of my eyes fraught with tears waiting to gain more weight and find a path, relieving me of the immense pain bottled up inside.

One way or the other, or another, I ended up sleepless. I tried to find a spot in my hotel room or someplace outside the window to hypnotise me through the night, helping me reminisce every moment I could have potentially not screwed up, but obviously did.

Simi had called and messaged frantically after I had disconnected the call, but I hadn't responded, despite knowing deep down inside that the fault was mine and that she hadn't done anything.

The ambience in the camp also reflected my mood. We were 2/4 on the win/loss column and it was the manner in which defeats had been handed out to us, that was the most perturbing fact. I, on the other hand, was shattered, sure that I wouldn't be playing in another match again.

Oscillating from one mental decision to another, I strolled dejectedly through the corridors of the Hyderabad hotel we stayed in, waiting for the next encounter against the Deccan Chargers the subsequent day. Uncertain whether I wanted another chance, the chance which was an uncertainty in itself, I didn't have it in me to see myself fail again -fail so miserably that I might not come back to the game ever. Fearing the fact that my love for the game might cease to exist, the ambiguity in my mind gradually started transforming into a strong belief that I didn't want another game. I wasn't fit enough to play for the Daredevils and an omission from the team would do me more good than otherwise.

Obviously, fate had other things in mind, as my name got announced in the list. Although it did feel good to hear my name again, I wondered how this was happening. Not able to combat this plethora of maddening thoughts, I walked up to Viru after the meet.

"I need to have a word with you Viru," I claimed, politely.

"Yes yes, go ahead," he said expressionless.

"Please tell me why am I in the team again.I mean, despite those horrible performances, how can I be in the team?I swear I am not telling anyone to pull strings for me. I do not understand what is going on." I said in the most pitiable tone Viru might ever have listened to.

"Oye!pull yourself together. What has happened? I want you to be in the team, that's why you are here," he said convincingly, though if he was doling out sarcasm again, I was not able to gather it.

"Viru bhai, please! How can I be in the team after those performances? Moreover, you know nothing about me to back me up. I am really having -doubts about my own abilities." I ended without a question, just letting my inner feelings out to someone I wasn't sure I should have.

He answered it with a smile and a long pause.

"Come with me," he said as he led me to the coffee house.

"Hot or cold coffee?" he asked.

"Nothing," I said.

"Hot or cold?" he got his point across like a mother nursing a small child unhappy about some happening in the house and then the child throwing food-related tantrums.

"Cold," the child obliged mummy.

"If you remember, I had told you to have faith, both in yourself and the God above. Where's the faith?" he asked.

I was quiet.

"Why are two failures bothering you so much? It's a long tough road and I have previously told you that you have talent. You are not God that you will come in and start scoring centuries from the first match itself. Even the best of them fail, and fail miserably. Failures are a part of sport, infact, a part of everything you intend to do in life, and this is reality, and not a movie, kid. I know I sound super-idealistic here but this sadly is the truth. You're what?Twentytwo-ish?so what's the hurry?Enjoy this game and learn as you go."

After a brief hiatus,he again added, "Is there someplace else you would rather be than play cricket?"

"No,Viru bhai! I love this game, it's what I am living for."

"Then you are too afraid of failures. You have just played a couple of matches and you want to see yourself performing. Do you know when Sachin got his first ODI century? After 79 ODIs." He told me a stat I already knew.

"I've heard you are an MBA, right?"

"Yes."

"You want to go back?"

"No."

"Then what is bugging you? If this is your life, do you have a choice other than to fail till you succeed?" he asked, rhetorically.

"No," I mumbled.

"Either be afraid and keep weighing your pros and cons about both cricket and your MBA or love this game like never before and see the way it shall love you back."

Trying to fathom what he said, all I did was nod in agreement.

"And you have been selected on merit, rest assured about that as long as I am the captain, and again, keep faith. That is the only thing that you shall have when you are down and out, which shall be many a time in your career, and if that wobbles, you have nothing."He said, as he sipped the last of his coffee.

I didn't really know whether I was supposed to speak after this and if I did, the question was, "What would Isay?" Finally, all I managed was a "Viru bhai,I can't even begin to express how to thank..."

"Don't say that, kid! Just believe!" he said, as he got up and left.

While I sipped my drink, I mused over what he had said. Yes, indeed it was failure I was scared of, and hence Iwas trying too hard every time, resulting in further failures. What was I afraid of? My meaningless MBA degree or the Holden job that would enslave me for life? I was better than this of course, I thought , resolute, promising myself that come what may, it was cricket that was life and even if it took a few lifetimes, I would pursue this dream.

Delhi Daredevils v/s Deccan Chargers was the next match. With respect to past records, we were the favourites, though on current form we had already lost seeing how they had won five on five in the tournament and they were currently the team to beat.

Tense no more, as I knew cricket was home now, for years to come,I'd now spend a lifetime on these grounds, playing, failing, trying and more importantly, tending to my love for this game.

I abruptly remembered my other love, Simi, to whom I had been unreasonable the day before. I had this intense urge to call her up, but players weren't allowed phones at the playing venue as they presumably got distracted. It was a different story that a few yards away from us were the prettiest cheer leaders gyrating in the skimpiest of clothing.

Anyhow, I saw Nelson using a laptop for some supposed "in-depth" analysis, which assisted in bringing forth strategic inputs right throughout the game, and helped us get the trouncing of our lives.

"Nelson, can I just use it for a minute. I have to see a statistic on Andrew. I worked out a plan for him, but it doesn't seem right now," I spoke his language so that refusal was not an option.

Eyeing me curiously, he gave me the laptop. "Hurry up. The match is about to be under way," he exclaimed.

I hurriedly logged on to an'sms'ing site and messaged an "I love you and I am sorry" to Simi. I cleared all the history and browsing content as I returned his laptop. I instantly felt lighter and the pangs of guilt that had been piercing me now subsided.

For the first time I was playing without any mental baggage, free to enjoy the game rather than worrying about what was to transpire next in my life. I was a cricketer for life, I confirmed to myself.

Batting first, catastrophe struck in the first over as both Viru and Gautam were dislodged to swinging peaches by Vaas. I felt a tense knot in my stomach and I was sure the whole dugout was sharing this feeling with me. Soon, after a mild fight back, we lost another couple of wickets, sending us reeling at 43/4 after seven overs.

The unnerving first seven overs had undone whatever calm I had rallied up. Joining Shashank at the crease, I nervously enquired about the game plan.

"It's twenty overs; so cautious aggression for now. One boundary an over apart from the singles and doubles for the next few overs."

"Alright, I'll take the boundary risk," I said, taking up the mantle.

"Ok," he said, as we punched our gloves and I walked to take strike.

Treating each ball on merit, respecting deliveries which deserved respect, and the others with disdain, I momentarily forgot I was playing the IPL. In my own zone, I proceeded briskly, ramping up a much- needed partnership. We moved along well till Shashank got out to a silly shot, trying to up the tempo. At 90/5 after twelve overs, Vinesh walked in.

"Keep taking singles and give me the strike," was the message from me as I was now feeling pretty sure about myself. We strode along at a healthy rate, with me getting boundaries at regular intervals. Drives, square cuts, flicks galore, I was playing as if in a dream. At the end of the sixteenth over, we got the signal from Viru to go for the jugular.

With my eye set in, I felt very similar to the day I'd pulverised the bowling machine. I ravaged each and every bowler with contempt in the next four overs. Contrary to my on-field frenzied batting display, my insides were calm, composed, and never over-awed by the situation. I knew today was the day to cash in.

92 not-out after the 19th over mark, with us comfortably placed at 175, there it was, the whole stadium brimming with

people chanting , clapping and spurring me on for a hundred. No matter how calm I tried to appear now, my heart was in my throat, ready to spring out of my mouth the first chance it got. Nothing had sunk in till now and frankly I didn't want it to. I wanted to get to the elusive 100 before I actually tried to realise what feat I had achieved.

Vaas ambled in the way he is known for, doing most of the bowling with his mind -the delivery is just a medium, they say, for him to complete his assassination. Pumped with adrenaline, with the hundred within a sniffing distance, on the verge of history in that IPL edition, I thought of getting over with it in a jiffy.

Once again it was the delivery that reaches hours after it's false initial promises. The innocuousness of which made my eyes light up, just like a whiff of oxygen sputtered into dying embers of coal, reigniting them once again. Consequently, I gave the ball a slog of a lifetime.

It was like a Diwali cracker, promising to explode, but just like some of them end up sounding like suppressed farts, I missed the line of the ball completely in the over excitement and the ball disarrayed the woodwork behind me.

The chants subsided and the stadium fell deathly silent, as I froze in the slog sweep position for what seemed like an eternity. Pulling myself together, I felt weighed down like a sponge soaked in water, as I began to walk the longest walk back to the dugout.

What ensued was a crescendo of applause which gradually transformed into an ovation of colossal proportions.It felt surreal, as if God had been videotaping my countless dreams, and had finally compiled it today to publish the best real-life motion-picture of all time. Shivers went down my spine as I removed my helmet and acknowledged the 30,000-strong crowd, kissing the

Delhi logo on my helmet. After all, it was this franchise that made me savour, for the first time, the taste of having a dream fulfilled.

All doubts that I had ever garnered felt ludicrous now. Of course, cricket was my calling, I thought while sitting there in the dugout during the break. The horde of people who congratulated me never appeared to finish, as I was the sensation of the day.

We won the match easily, as the 182 we piled up proved to be a mammoth of a score, and chasing under lights, they never had a decent chance anyways. The congratulations just didn't seem to stop.

"So, Mr.Champion," chuckled Viru, who was in a great mood after a much-needed victory.

"Viru bhai, at least you don't pull my leg. It's just one game, and all thanks to you," I said candidly.

"What! Me? You were there, batting at the crease, not me. Anyway kid, you'll have many such moments. Don't let it get to your head," he said and rightly so, as I did need grounding at these moments of intense flattery that I was subjected to.

"Thank you again, Viru bhai!" I said, to which he smiled and left.

Indeed, I thought, I had to keep myself grounded. I remembered what had happened after the mediocre success I had enjoyed after the first match, I had hit rock bottom in the next two.Oscillating like a sine wave, I didn't want to hit nadir again.

Back to the hotel, the TV channels had already started their customary extolment, as they do with regard to anyone who shines, even briefly, dishing out shoddily-compiled statements for cheap journalistic thrills. This time, the subject of the eulogy was yours truly. The ridiculousness of the India TVs and the Aaj Taks, as usual crossed their own previously set limits, by the "Ye dekhiye, kal ke Sachin Tendulkar," and "MBA ya cricketer, har jagah bichha diya hai apna jalwa: Vineet Grover." I had to isolate myself from this madness till the next match, rather, I had to concentrate on the rest of the season that lay ahead, of which I was now surely a member of.

As I entered the room, I called up Simi, the first thing.

"Hi," she said indifferently.

"I am very sorry, Simi."

"Ok." she replied coldly.

"No, I really am. I was devastated and I misdirected my negative emotions towards you. I am an idiot," I clarified lamely.

"Okay," she wasn't going to give in any time soon, I thought.

"I love you Simi, a lot that is, please forgive me," I tried again.

"Congrats for today, by the way," she said, as I saw touches of warmth in her voice, for which I loved her so much.

"I am dying to meet you. I'll be in Delhi tomorrow, can we meet at night?" I asked.

"Ok," she said again.

I made lame conversation for another ten minutes, by which time she had also started contributing to it. With a sorry and an I love you placed strategically after every two minutes of the conversation, like a true MBA, I got her to reciprocate within twenty. The MBA in me hadn't died, I thought foolishly, as we spoke for another hour.

The dream had taken flight.

CHAPTER 9

Almost There

"Impossible is just a big word thrown around by small men who find it easier to live in the world they've been given than to explore the power they have to change it. Impossible is not a fact. It's an opinion. Impossible is not a declaration. It's a dare. Impossible is potential. Impossible is temporary. Impossible is nothing."

— *Mohammad Ali*

After that day, there was no looking back. Like a man who had found his calling and who exuded confidence, I never doubted myself again. The IPL was a mediocre success for the Delhi Daredevils but a spectacular one for me. Four fifties at astounding strike rates, a couple of breathtaking, lifesaving thirties and being a more than handy bowler who was at his best during the death overs was what made me an indispensible asset to the team.

I was now one of the main stays of the Delhi formation, being in the 'form of a lifetime,' as Viru would describe it.

"Use it to the hilt till it withers away, boy," he'd say, patting my back.

Team meetings saw me as the cynosure, which translated into me being the fallback guy during the matches. I was the one who was relied upon to weather the storm in the toughest of situations. Nelson and Viru both exhibited immense faith in me, giving me the self-belief, which, combined with oodles of luck, saw me executing each innings with pinpoint perfection.

Being named the 'Emerging Player of the Tournament' and adding this feat with the three 'Man of the Match' trophies I bagged along the way, I was now a known name in the Indian Premier League circuit and a bigger one in the Delhi cricketing circles. Money, the last thing which attracted me in this pursuit of a dream, was more than what all interns at Holden put together would earn in a year.

The sad part of this surreal experience was that we got knocked out in the semi-finals in a cliffhanger of a match. It was a heart breaking moment, as Dilshan and I put up a brave show, but we still fell short by a few runs. It hurt badly, but the Emerging Player of the Tournament was of course, more than a consolation prize, a stamp of being the most promising youngster amongst a number of other accolades. Unofficially, I was the first in queue of many talented blokes knocking at the doors of the selectors for the coveted team India cap.

I had fallen in love with Simi, all over again. On the day before the semi-finals, I had asked her, going down on my knee, with a huge lustrous solitaire in one hand, to be my better half, and that I would love her, each day every hour, for the remainder of my life, more than ever before.

She had smiled and we had kissed, along the Marine Drive in Mumbai at 1 o'clock in the morning.

"It was always a yes from me, and I think dad also knows about us. He drops subtle hints at me, I feel," she winked, as we kissed again.

"I'll talk to him the day I become an established cricketer! What say?" I asked her.

"That should do just fine, my Tendulkar, anyway I'm just twenty-two now, you pedophile," she joked.

"Not funny, huh!" I said, as I held her close in my arms and we gazed at the waves hitting the rocks with ferocity, ironically casting forth the most picturesque panorama on this almost perfect romantic evening.

❖ ❖ ❖

The most awaited clash of the year was only a month away; India v/s Pakistan, a five one-day international match series followed by a two test match series. Anticipating a call, I was practicing without respite, working on every nuance of my game. I was a mild national sensation by now, with every discussion, every talk show panel, and cricketing articles in dailies mentioning my name. The common thread across them was that they all expected me to find a place in the fourteen-member Team India squad. Opinions differed, as some argued that IPL was no barometer to judge a player of hisskills and without Ranji credentials, a performance there did not merit a place in Team India. But the majority rubbished these claims and vouched for the newest star on the Indian cricketing scene. They could love me or hate me, but they could not ignore me, such was the power of my performance in the IPL.

High on this success, I made a conscious effort to not let my game slack off, because unlike before, there would be expectations from me now. In a cricket-crazed nation, I had missed not one eye, and just like this nation catapults you to fame, the shame associated with failure is equally and unabashedly manifested in every action of your fans. This fact I knew very well.

I had already received offers for TV commercials, albeit from smaller brands, which I had refused to take up, both on account of concentrating on my game at the moment, and not wanting to dilute my brand equity, that is, if I became a bigger brand ambassador down the line. I still remembered a major part of my marketing lessons from the first year of my MBA classes, and they helped.

It was while speaking with a few college friends, discussing college gossip, when the mention of how the Dean was noticeably mad at my where abouts, came up. Feeling a little guilty about how I had left college without any prior intimation and formal procedure, and to top it, how my TV appearances would now have made everyone aware of the fast ones I had pulled on them the whole time, made me feel a bit ashamed.

First and foremost, I called up the Dean of my college. The Dean was a tall, dark, moustached man. His posture was erect and face weathered, eyes dark, and looked like they were brimming with knowledge, with mild dark circles encircling them, as if they were guardians of that knowledge. He wore thin-rimmed glasses and was always dressed in immaculate formal clothes which gave him a supremely suave look. His face, ironically, demanded and earned respect, both at the same time. I had already started to feel a little nervous as I dialed his phone number.

"Hello?" came his crisp, somber voice.

"Hello sir, this is Vineet here."

"Oh, hello, Mr. Vineet. So finally you have got the time to call." He spoke with copious sarcasm.

"I am extremely sorry sir, I never knew how to face you."

"Son, you are a cricketer now. So much fear will not be of any help."

"I know sir, hence today I summoned up enough courage to apologise for leaving college midway," I spoke with a genuine penitence.

"It is ok. It's better late than never. So do you wish to withdraw admission, or complete your education sometime next year?" he inquired with a concern I had actually anticipated, owing to the genuinely nice man he was.

"Sir, I would love to, but sadly I cannot attend classes.I sure can study by myself and appear for the examinations, if that is an option?" I asked expectantly.

"Hmm...as a Dean I cannot treat you as an exception," he spoke sternly.

"I understand, sir," I said, with a tinge of self-pity in my voice expecting to melt his usually inviolable stand on issues.

There was a long pause during the duration of which I felt really uncomfortable.

"Ok! I shall discuss this with the faculty and let you know of our decision, but don't be too optimistic," finally, he spoke, breaking the barbed silence.

"Thank you so much sir! For everything," I said.

"Yes, and best of luck for your career and do drop by someday to meet your classmates."

"Surely sir, I'll visit soon," I promised.

❖ ❖ ❖

Life was getting luxurious with the amount of money that had poured in. I was a multimillionaire, courtesy the IPL. With more expected to come in, and in my attempt to appear as a worthy future husband, when I'd ask for Simi's hand from her father, whenever that would be, I figured it would be safe to invest the money in a house. Along with that, a car also seemed an immediate necessity.

After a little research, I zeroed in on a Honda City and finalised it after Simi's approval, even though it was like scrap in front of her BMW. By now even my grandmother, who did not understand much of cricket had realized that her grandson had achieved something rather big. I was chastised for having completely forgotten her since I had started appearing on TV, something for which I knew I was guilty. When the conversations turned light, she told me, how everyday some or the other lady from the neighbourhood visited her, subtly slipping in the matrimonial credentials of their daughters/sisters/sister's sisters or daughter's daughters. We shared quite a few chuckles over these conversations.

With Simi in my life, staying with grandma was not an option any more. For my grandma would have been a little shocked to see her grandson being visited by a young lady. To avoid the awkwardness I knew I had to look for a new place to stay. But I did visit grandma from time to time, often gifting her household necessities which made her old-age a little more comfortable. The thought of introducing Simi to my grandma, once I was sure of when we would marry which depended upon my future as a cricketer, also lingered at the back of my mind.

Realising that there was no decent house available for the sum my bank account boasted of, I decided to merely rent a better place and think of the house a wee bit later.

I found a decent home, in a posh colony in Vasant Vihar, a one bedroom, hall, kitchen, for a reasonable rent. It was good enough for me, a bachelor. Simi helped me set it up tastefully, giving it a look which made it evident that a female had effectuated the interiors. I, though, didn't mind it as it reminded me of her when she wasn't with me.

❖ ❖ ❖

My expectations of a call for the high-profile Indo-Pak series had gradually plummeted because I'd heard rumours that selectors do not select star performers immediately as it supposedly gets on to their heads. They look for consistent performers, who have performed for many seasons before they are honoured with that elusive India cap. Still, just knowing that a future which had only cricket featuring in it, lay ahead, was more than comforting, and I knew my time would come.

Feasting on my half-fried eggs and fresh orange juice, I was lazing around on a surprisingly pleasant Saturday morning. I sat on my couch, going over the movie collection on my laptop, looking forward to a power-packed testosterone-filled Arnold Schwarzeneger-featuring blockbuster Saturday and expecting the showroom manager to call any moment, for the handover of my sparkling white Honda City.

After finishing with Commando, I had just started with Terminator 2, when somewhere around noon, the manager, who sounded like a slick man, and spoke in a friendly girlish voice, informed me about the availability of the car. I was to collect it anytime I wished, he stated.

Thanking him I called up Simi, to accompany me to pick up the vehicle. I quickly slipped into a pair of jeans and was about to leave when I got another call.

"Hello?"

"Hello, is that Vineet?" asked an old, tired voice, of a man who wouldn't have been any younger than fifty.

"Yes, this is Vineet."

"Vineet, I am calling from the BCCI office. You have been selected for the fourteen-member team for the next series."

Numb, flabbergasted and dumbfounded. I could have blacked out any moment.

"Yes, sir. Thank you," I said with a lump in my throat as large as an overgrown plum.

"Please report at the BCCI Office tomorrow at 10 a.m." He spoke suavely, rather too suavely for a government official.

"Yes sir, I shall be there." I struggled to form legitimate speech, as tears had already started rolling down my cheeks.

I wiped them off as overwhelming emotions engulfed me. It was not about happiness anymore. Happiness was an emotion very diminutive in front of what I felt. If there was a time when the phrase "as if the world had come to a screeching halt" could have been used, it had to be this.

It was precisely a year back when I had felt the intense need to be associated with this game, standing in the grounds of Infotech, after losing a game that we should have won. Nightmares had haunted me for days altogether, pushing me to pursue this mirage, which I had then shunned as a childish fantasy.

Then making it to one of best B-schools of the country, enrolling with a cricket club just for kicks, where I realised my performances were no fluke and were more a harvest of the God-sent talent,the months of intense labour, when everything else took a backseat, the day when I gave up my exams and the prestigious MBA degree for the selection camp, the most pivotal day of my life, which then lead to the most mercurial and erratic journey of a lifetime, including the most crushing lows and the most awe-inspiring highs all flashed in my mind. All this had finally culminated at the peak where I stood now, like a maverick who had defied every possible norm and fought every probable difficulty, that indicated that I should not pursue this illusion laden dream. I was amongst the lucky few who deviated from the customary path, and could actually claim to have lived a dream.

Fraught with incredulousness, I started my bike as I left for Simi's.

Still lost in my fantasy world, I snaked through the traffic, letting the throttle loose with my Bullet belting out rpms unheard of, weaving, bobbing and having an expression of eternal joy pasted on my face.

CHAPTER 10

The Nightmare

"Hope is a good thing, maybe the best of things,

and no good thing ever dies."

— Andy Dufrense in 'The Shawhank Redemption'

My eyes refused to admit the blinding sunlight that the windows allowed in, as the curtains, crisp white with a mild floral design, hung tautly, parted on the pelmet. Adjusting to the glaring light, I somehow managed to open my eyes.

The curtains looked different somehow. They didn't belong to my house, I thought, as I still battled to keep my eyes from fluttering rapidly. The brain worked exceptionally slower than normal and there felt an alarming gap between what the eyes be held, and what the brain processed.

It took a couple of minutes to dawn upon me that I was in a hospital room. All the sophisticated equipment stood beside the wall, behind my head, so I had not been able to figure out the significance of the room earlier. The insane amount of white in the room was creepy and the eerie silence was somewhat unnerving. I felt too lethargic to even bat my eyelids, let alone move my body.

I tried to recall any chronology of events that could give me the reason for my presence in that room, thus pressurising my sluggish brain cells for the second time in a matter of minutes, but no answers were elicited. I tried again, harder this time, but failed miserably.

Disoriented, I became a little panicky. I was Vineet Grover, an MBA from FMS, well, half an MBA and a cricketer who had been awarded the emerging player of the tournament award at the IPL, I recalled. I felt a part of my misery alleviated as I realized, I remembered something at least. I tried one final time to recall anything that could explain the reason of my being in that hospital bed. Nil. Nada. Zilch.

Anxiousness had now reached miserable levels as I wanted to go out of there desperately. I tried to sit up to leave, but a searing pain emerged from my lower back right up to my neck as I winced in extreme discomfort. Something macabre had happened, I was sure by then. No amount of beating, unless with a metal object, could induce such bloodcurdling pains.

Had I been beaten by someone? I tried to resort to the activity of thinking again, and it failed me one more time.

Out of instinct, I launched a frantic search operation looking for some sign of a button, to call someone, which I found in the form of a cordless plastic box. I extended the antenna, just to be sure, as I pressed the button a couple of times.

After a brief moment, the door opened as a woman peeped in and then gradually let herself into the room

"Hello, Mr Vineet, so how are you feeling? Finally you are up!" said the woman in white (again), feigning a plastic smile she seemed to have practised to perfection.

"Why am I here?" I asked.

This question seemed to change her facial expressions, as the contrived smile betrayed her emotions. She left immediately without saying a word.

Something very morbid was in store for me, I was sure as I quickly flung across the blanket atop me to check my limbs, finding them tucked safely inside the robe I wore. I was, by God's grace fine, contrary to the ominous signals I had been getting and hence fearing the worst, thanks to what I had seen in many a Hindi movie, where the hero found one of his limbs missing after such episodes of oddities in a hospital.

Just as I checked every limb on my body simultaneously making failed attempts at recalling any plausible reasons for me being there, the door opened and a man, more erudite-looking than the nurse, probably due to his suave, thin-rimmed glasses, receding hairline, educated face, a coat whiter than anything else in the room, and a stethoscope straight from the movies, stepped in.

"Hello, Vineet," he spoke in a suave, thick educated voice, removing his spectacles which he placed in the pocket of his coat, with a smile which looked far more genuine than that on the nurse's face.

"So, how are you?" he asked me the same question.

"How am I supposed to know that? You tell me!" I yelped like a dog.

"Oh, and before that, please tell me why am I here?" I was now a little impatient by the awkward niceness all around me, for no apparent reason.

I saw his expression change the same way the nurse's had. I was sweating profusely by now. What was so wrong with what I had asked? I wondered.

"You do not remember anything about how you got here?" He now spoke with an expression so intense, it made me miserable.

I could have given a sarcastic reply, the urge for which was immense, but I let it pass and answered with a simple "No."

"Can you tell me something about yourself?" he asked, reminding me of my MBA interviews. Yes I remembered them too, and I felt a tinge of happiness.

"I am Vineet Grover, a cricketer by profession, a half MBA from FMS Delhi. I stay at …" I stopped.

"I stay at Sat…" I stopped again, as I knew I didn't remember much and tried to cerebrate, but unsurprisingly, my mind went blank.

There was a mild smile on the doctor's face by now. Was the sadistic bastard enjoying the pathetic state I was in?I wondered.

"Why are you smiling?" I asked, hoping for an answer that reassures me of my mental soundness.

"Please tell me more about yourself," he said, ignoring my question.

"I have been brought up in an Army background, but my parents passed away when I was pretty young," I spoke as I felt stabs across my abdomen as I spoke the dreaded statement. Even though I didn't recall where I stayed, this nightmare was still as clear as it was on the day it had happened.

"I did my schooling from Army School, then completed my engineering and worked with Infotech Limited… heck what's the point of all this?" I asked, now visibly irritated.

"Nothing, Vineet, I think you should take rest now," he said, with a mellow grin again, as it seemed his experiment bore the results he wanted.

"You still haven't answered why I am here!" I asked, itching to strangle him by now.

"You had a small accident. But you shall be fine soon," his smiles were now getting on to my nerves.

"Since when have I been here and would you please spare your precious time to elaborate my accident for me," I said, with intended sarcasm as it had by now become unbearable to remain in the realms of uncertainty.

"It's been four days," he said as he sat down again, holding tightly onto his knees.The poor guy seemed weak.

"You were riding a bike when you had an accident." He spoke with minimal elaboration.

"Please tell me more?" I asked again.

"Listen Vineet, I shall tell you everything, it's just that you have to give it some time. You know everything you need to as of now, and Simi should be here any moment. You want to meet her, don't you?" he said, enticing me like I was a small kid being offered a chocolate.

Simi! I recalled. The love of my life…Smiling, chirpy, cheerful and insanely pretty. Yes, I remembered her and my heart bate faster in the anticipation of seeing her.

"Yes, I do, when'll she be here?" I asked with childish curiosity, possibly satiating the intent behind his last statement.

"Any moment now," he was smiling again. The conniving bastard, I thought.

"Which hospital is this?" I asked one last question out of curiosity.

"The Appollo," he said, peeping in from the door with the rest of his body outside the room.

Unnerved after knowing I had been there for four days with no clue of how, what, when and why, I was going brainsick.

I adjusted my posture, lying more comfortably as I gazed at the ceiling aimlessly, a flurry of thoughts crossing my mind, recollecting everything I possibly could, leaving major blanks at places, perturbing me, making me put more pressure on by brain cells, till every single time, I turned frustrated and gave up.

The door opened almost silently as there stood the girl who brightened my face. Simi, looking prettier than before, as had been the norm with her since I'd started loving her, came in with a huge bouquet of flowers, and the cutest smile that made her face seem more radiant than ever before.

In with her, entered a wave of fragrance that was a relief from the conventional smell of antiseptic and medicines that my room had initially reeked of.

Simi came up and kissed me, as she placed the bouquet next to the hospital equipment.

"So, how do you feel?"she asked,as her eyebrows twitched with an expression which was neither one of happiness nor gloomy.

"Tired of answering that one baby, but I feel I'm ok, at least those were the vibes the doctor gave me. I do tend to forget things but the doctor didn't seem too bothered," I spoke casually.

She held my hand and clutched it tightly as I could see her eyes getting moist.

"Simi don't cry yaar. I'm okay now. See, all is good, I'm here talking to you!" I said.

"No. I'm alright," she spoke as she wiped her eyes with the back of her hand, forcing a teeny smile. "Doc doesn't say what happened at the accident. What happened?" I asked her.

"Nothing. As you were coming to pick me up, you must've been driving fast and you jumped a red light and…" she started to sob then, unable to complete the sentence.

"Don't cry, yaar, forget it!. I don't want to know what happened," I said, more to console her. Actually, the need to know the truth had now grown manifold.

"No no, listen!" she braved on.

"Then this SUV hit you at tremendous speed. Eyewitnesses said you were flung in the air and by the time I came to know, you were already in the hospital. I told them not to inform your grandmother as I thought she'd not be able to take it. When I saw you, I passed out. It was that bad," she was still crying but in a toned-down manner, wiping off the tears just as they streamed down her perfectly-shaped cheeks.

"You have been in coma for four days," she told me.

"You know that a coma can last from days to weeks and in worst cases, years, and the outcomes are pathetic in most cases," she explained.

"Yes, I know. I am lucky," I said, still unable to take in the fact that I had been in coma for four days!

"I'd sit outside the ICU all day, praying, hoping for the doctor to say something positive, give some hint -but you know how they are when it comes to revealing emotions. They can be absolute statues," she said with her voice breaking at several instances and with a face that screamed of helplessness.

"I love you and I am so sorry to put you through all this, Simi," I felt sad inside, at the same time, still exasperated at the description of the accident and the four-day coma fact.

"Today morning you came out of coma but were writhing in pain and they medicated you and shifted you here. I took a bath today after four days and came running," she said with a hint of embarrassment and a smile that made me want to kiss her.

I again tried to up myself to do it, but it pained miserably and I had to lie down on the bed again. She understood my intent and leaned forward to kiss me again on my forehead.

"Lips," I said, with a smile.

"It's a hospital, you horny man!" she said, albeit kissing me on the lips which felt a little moist as I inhaled the fragrance of her strawberry lip gloss.

"Does the BCCI office know of this?" I asked.

"Yes, they do, and your name has been omitted from the list for now," she said nonchalantly.

"But why? I am okay! The series is still a good twenty days away!" I said.

"Yes, and how are you going to play with both legs fractured at multiple points?" she spoke, as a matter of fact.

"What?" I spoke aghast, as I hurriedly checked under the huge robe I wore. My legs were plastered heavily, and strangely, somehow, I hadn't noticed or felt the plaster. It felt as if a thousand needles were piercing me, as I discovered it was actually not an innocuous accident.

"It's okay baby. Fractures take barely a couple of months to heal. You'll be ready to roll in no time!" she said, maintaining a hopeful look on her face.

I do not recollect much after this conversation - just that I felt really weak, and having a feeling that I would pass out any moment.

It felt like the sleep of a life time. I felt rejuvenated and refreshed with the whiteness of the room still as sparkling as when I had last got up.

The sudden need to know how long I had slept, absorbed me. I rung the bell and waited. A nurse entered, prettier than the one before, though with the same artificial smile lighting her face. She greeted me.

"What day is it?" I asked her still struggling to be fully mentally alert, the same drowsiness engulfing me after the false initial feeling of being reenergised.

"Sunday," she said, as I realised that the day did not mean anything to me.

"How long did I sleep ?" I rephrased.

"Not much. One and a half days, sir," she said, while doing her chores of checking the equipment placed next to me, from which pipes emerged and ended under a huge bandage with multiple inlets, presumably into my blood stream.

"One and a half day is not much?" I asked with surprise.

"What do you think I am, Kumbhkaran?!" I added, although later it seemed uncalled-for, as she was a mere nurse.

"Sir, it is normal for coma patients to sleep for such periods of time," she said, reminding me of the coma I had just come out of.

"Can you please just call the doctor?" I said, purely out of disgust at the lack of empathy shown by the nurse. I felt weak; I shouldn't talk so much, I thought. Exhausted, as if every ounce of energy had been sucked out, all from a mere three-minute jabber, I felt I was sinking, everything around me feeling hazy.

The white surroundings were not as well-defined as they were five minutes back, as I phased out once again.

I got up after another 30 hours, at least that is what the doctor claimed as he sat on a chair in front of me, identically dressed as all the previous times. Dazed by all the medication, I was unsure whether what I witnessed was real or a mere figment of my imagination while still fast asleep. This constant juggling between the realms of reality and fantasy was driving me mad.

"This happens, Vineet , no need to panic!" he said as I almost shouted at him for not telling me what exactly I was suffering from, as these 30-hour naps were getting to me.

"Do not patronise me! No one sleeps for days altogether, and then when he asks what's wrong, he doesn't want to hear 'you're alright'," I said, not being able to take anymore of his supposed bullshit.

"I am not, Vineet . What you are going through is normal for someone with a head injury. Please do not put a lot of pressure on yourself. You came out of coma within four days, which was the best news you could have asked for. These phases of sleep shall occur.You have no reason to panic," he said, making more sense than usual.

"I can't remember a lot of things. So, how bad is my head injury?" I asked, citing this as the best possible time to elicit answers because for once, he had stopped smiling and was talking logically.

"Initially we were doubtful about you, when we brought you in, that is.It was a horrific sight, to be frank, but you're a strong man, and were up in four days. Plus you seem to forget only the accident and tend to recall all the long-term memories which, again,is a sign that you are fine. Head injuries caused due to accidents tend to make you forget the period when the accident took place, hence your situation is normal," he said and smiled. His continued smiling is what irritated me most.

"You have severely injured your spine, too, which was the most scary part, but since you have been moving your limbs fine, I guess all is good," he smiled (yet)again.

"Yes, I guess, it's all..." I stopped.

Albeit the slow cerebral activity, my mind pointed out something strange.

I tried to feel them -my legs and the plaster that is usually too heavy to not notice or not feel, but I felt nothing. For the first time in so many days, I made a conscious effort, to get some sort of sensory signal from my legs that they were alive, something that I had taken for granted, but there was no response.

I tried to get up but couldn't, with the same pain surging, wanting to make me shriek.

"What are you doing?!Lie down!" demanded the doctor.

"Doc, I havn't felt my legs in days, I can't feel the plaster!" I trembled while speaking, shaking uncontrollably. How had I missed it? I blanked out for a moment.

"What? What are you saying?" he asked again, more out of ritual than because he hadn't heard what I had said.

"I cannot feel my fucking legs, don't you get it,you retard!" I spoke, hysterical, spitting saliva as I shouted like a child who had lost his mother, not that I hadn't experienced that, too.

He got up and undid my robe as I lay there shaking uncontrollably, with me still under a spell of convulsions. He pinched my thigh.

"You feel something?" he asked me.

I kept howling, tearless, on the brink of insanity, wanting to retaliate violently, but not capable of even moving a pin.

He pinched with more intensity, which still didn't elicit any sensory feeling. None, whatsoever.

I began mouthing profanities, as tears eluded me. My back was killing me by all the jerks I subjected myself to, but the pain of being sensation-less and paralysed had killed me, almost.

I blacked out one more time.

For the next few days, I would howl, shout, cry and blabber out incoherent stuff understood by no one. A nurse was permanently stationed there to observe me as the doctors were afraid I might take an extreme step as patients of paralysis usually try to. I would usually black out after a brief session of intense hollering or a sleep-inducing drug would be introduced into my body so that I didn't suffer any further, both mentally and physically.

The pain in the back had aggravated due to the violent movements and it took more quantities of morphine than the last time to put me to sleep. Time had lost meaning, as had my life. The intensities of my wails reduced, as my body was left with no more vitality to revolt. I felt more like a ninety year old patient, breathing his last, whimpering, mumbling, and talking to himself. On the brink of madness, I had lost all power to understand and comprehend anything that happened around me.

I didn't know when I got up, I didn't care either. During one of these never-ending cycles phasing in and out of life, I woke up to find a nurse and Simi sitting beside me. The nurse was reading some shady newspaper and Simi slept with her head on a table.

I didn't want to get up, and wished I was dead, and the tears that eluded me last time, came out as if suddenly let loose.. I wept noisily and it caught the attention of both of them.

Simi jerked up and ran up to me, hugging me.

I cried and mumbled and blabbered, to all of which Simi said,

"I love you and I am here with you baby."

Words were inconsequential and no amount of them felt even minutely soothing. It all felt like a lie that was being said to pacify me, which, to my repulsion, was actually true.

I would get violent at times, calling names to everyone in the vicinity, yelling at them to leave the room, There was just one constant throughout -Simi -who tried and usually failed to calm me down. I would only calm down once I passed out or was sapped of every ounce of energy in my already decrepit body.

No one ever even tried to tell me that my paralysis was a transient state and that it would go away, or that with time and a lot of practice, I might be able to walk again, as they thought I was paralysed for life.

Tears would finish, but not my weeping. Crying tearless is by far the worst physical affliction that a person can go through. The eyes puff up and the inflammation feels excruciating, because you want to stop crying but you can't. I phased in and out regularly, crying, always finding Simi there. The only thing that actually stopped me from committing suicide, a thought which frequented my mind at a disturbing rate, was Simi, sitting there, trying to give false promises about how we would go to the best doctors, where technologies unheard-of in India have come up.

She would keep searching for doctors on the internet, naively make ISD calls, all to know that this had no treatment, eliciting another mild session of weeping from me.

It had been twenty days since I had passed an hour without shedding tears, unless sleeping, which was either induced by utter exhaustion or a drug. Since there was no nastier news remaining, the doctor had also apprised me about the collateral damage I had suffered -apart from me being paralysed. He told me that these phases of sleep sometimes take months to get over with, an aftermath of the head injury;the same reason why my brain had gone considerably slower than before. He mentioned it as 'slightly slow,' but as time passed, I knew what 'slightly' meant, when Simi's longer sentences now took time to be understood.

The hysterics had subsided but the crying hadn't. I would stare aimlessly at the television -irrespective of the display on it, with my face blank. Blank, expressionless interrupted only by streams of tears every now and then. I tried hard to divert my mind, muse over little happenings of my life but the string of thought-formation always took me to a place where I realised the importance of what I had lost -my legs.

The mental pain only got exacerbated whenever anything even remotely related to cricket would be shown on television. The nightmares of me trying to play cricket only to realise my paralytic self would jolt me up from sleep many times.

❖ ❖ ❖

"Staying in the hospital is doing you no good, baby," Simi said one day, as I was again under a spell of silent weeping, waging a battle against the truth that had befallen me, after I had heard a ward boy discuss the last match heroics of some new guy who had probably taken my place in Team India.

"Where do I go? I have no one," I asked her like a homeless street mendicant, with nauseating levels of self-pity.

"Why are you talking like this? I am here with you, today, tomorrow, always. Do not ever say that again," she said in a dominating tone.

"Let's not kid ourselves, Simi, you have your whole life in front of you. You don't want it to be spent with a paralytic," I said again, though leaving the tones of self-pity out.

"I don't think of it that way. I think of it as spending my life with someone I love so much, he can never ever fathom," she said, blinded by tears.

I sat quietly, trying to control what would be another of those crying fits, my throat was one big lump and I detested God for doing this to me.

I felt like I had been dropped from the seventh heaven, right into the dungeons of hell.

I actually pitied Simi for what God had done to her, forcing her to stay with a handicapped person for the rest of her life. The crying started and did not stop until I drained out my glands, unable to produce anymore tears.

A month had passed and the doctors were contemplating discharging me as I'd become more stable now. There was a mild cheer in the air as Hardik was coming down to India to meet me.

He'd been informed about the mishap by Simi a week back and he immediately rushed back from France, where he was currently working on an onsite visit for Infotech Ltd. After a long time, I had allowed the nurse to freshen me up and I wore a new black t-shirt. Simi had also come decked up more than usual as we sat there making small talk, waiting for him.

With Simi in the midst of one of her many motivational speeches, trying to chalk out the perfect career for me, Hardik entered the room.

Managing a smile, like his cheerful self, I noticed his eyes red and swollen. I hated myself more, for putting my loved ones through this period of mental bleeding.

"What's up bro?" he asked, as came up and hugged me. He exchanged greetings with Simi while settling onto the chair next to Simi's.

"Your friend is handicapped," I spoke with a smile after seeing my best friend after such a long time.

"Oh shut up, saale! I've cried enough," he said, while showing me the back of his hand to indicate the slap he would not mind giving me if I didn't stop those pitiful statements.

"There will be no more crying," he said, as he held my hand and looked at me with the most loving eyes.

After a brief conversation, as the discussion veered towards my accident, I couldn't help my self, and I started crying again, periodically snivelling; making mucus-laden sounds.

Hardik tried to say something but Simi stopped him as she knew this was something I had to do; I had to let all the infliction out of my system in the form of tears till I actually stopped pitying myself. They sat there with their hands in mine, as I let the stream of sorrow out of my eyes.

If dealing with my paralysis was not enough, I had to deal with the socially pitiable and contemptible life I was dragging Simi into. Unlike what I had presumed, her father never questioned her decision of being with a cripple throughout her life, readily accepting every decision she made, something that was beyond my comprehension.

Under fits of self-loathing and pity, I would snap at Simi, occasionally telling her to leave me alone, but she never got agitated, as if she was the angel God had sent to take care of me after making me the subject of his experiment horrendously gone wrong.

Her father would, in fact, frequently visit the orphan who had recently been crippled, for whom, sadly for him, his daughter had fallen. I felt sad for both of them, but maybe, just maybe God had some semblance of compassion for me, I thought, because had Simi left me, I would have, without second thoughts, not felt inclined to have lived another day.

My grandmother, the only close relative I had, was saved the shock, as I told her that the state was transient and I would be perfectly fine, though it would take a few years. She herself was not in the best of health, having already undergone two bypass surgeries and with her Punjabi habit of downing ghee even at the age of eighty, I knew the false hope of walking again would outlast her living days. At least sheshould live peacefully, I thought.

❖ ❖ ❖

I still remember the day when I was introduced to my wheelchair for the first time. That day I realised how I had taken life for granted, every single day of my life

I would be the subject of pity now, subject to the "you first" in queues, a special VIP section for me everywhere I went, reminding me, just in case I momentarily forgot, that I was a cripple.

Simi stood there describing my wheelchair, it's features that were way better than any wheelchair in the market, and Hardik was engrossed in reading the manual, voicing out some of the important excerpts from it, as if it was a new gadget to be drooled upon, forgetting that, at the end of it, it was indeed a wheelchair, a wheelchair for the handicap, that was me.

I did not want to, I so did not want to, but I just couldn't help myself from breaking down as I moved onto the wheelchair. It was unbearable. A young lad with dreams in his eyes, who was meant to touch the skies, now sat on a wheelchair, wasted waist below, his muscles useless, and he himself crying like an extremely vulnerable child.

Simi was usually strong, rather very strong, as I had hardly ever seen a tear in her eye when with me, but somehow today, after two months, she at last crumbled, maybe the reason being that she was, after all, human. As she sat down and hugged me, we cried together, and in the confines of our misery, a misery that was mine and one which she had accepted as her own with both arms open, we came even closer to each other. Hardik stood there speechless, but he joined us after a minute, hugging us, and giving us the strength we needed.

I felt miserable for what God had donc to this little girl, whose only mistake in life had been to fall in love with a guy for whom the word unlucky would be a conspicuously gross understatement.

After six long months of coming to terms with my crippled self and Simi's periodic inspirational speeches, I had now lived to learn with my difficulties.

After the fourth month of the accident, Simi had asked me to marry her as she wanted to be with me all the time, taking care of me.

I was an unemployed cripple, but the ego of the man inside me was still as strong as of the man I was before.

"I want to make a career first, Simi, so that I feel worthy of marrying you, otherwise I would die of guilt," I had explained.

"How does it matter? Marriage will give us the license to stay together, then you can pick up a job and so will I.Where is the problem in this? Don't become so filmy all of a sudden, Vineet," she answered casually.

"I am not being filmi, I am ok staying alone, I am over that initial phase of crying. It's July again. My new session will be starting. I'll finish my MBA and the day I land up with a job, we will get married," I explained.

"Who can argue with you? Whatever!"she threw her hands in the air as she went into the kitchen to prepare lunch.

The life back to college was refreshing, a distraction of sorts from my mundane, maimed life. My batch mates were my seniors now. The welcome back that was given to me was that of a hero, and a special party was organised in my honour. It felt heartwarming to hear the Dean speak for a couple of minutes on the courage I had depicted, to be back to college after an incident which could have broken the best of us.

For the first time after the accident I felt good, the handicap didn't feel as bad as before, since I was on course to live a life of normalcy once again. The life I despised, the life I mocked before being a cricketer was the one I strived to get back to. Situations change perspectives, everything is relative; these sentences started making apt sense in my life.

Although I could easily see the difference in my cerebral sharpness before the accident and now, yet, it was not the question of high IQ, it was the question of not breaking, of not giving up, of striving continuously, of putting to practice the learnings of millions of inspirational stories Simi had recited to me.

Even if I felt like giving up, just the thought of Simi would spur me on, her smile, and the fact I'd see her in the evening gave me a reason cogent enough not to let go. She had given up everything for me, the least I could do for her was to not give up.

I was sweating bullets as the placements arrived. Although I did have a strong CV by now, with the credentials of a national cricketer against my name, yet, since mobility was an issue, I knew most companies would not fancy me as a strong candidate.

I got placed with a decent public sector company. Although the salary wasn't that handsome, when the profile on offer, the reimbursements, house and vehicle when added to it, it summed up to a deal which satisfied me. I felt a little jealous to see a douche bag get placed with Holden, bagging an astronomical compensation. It hurt to reminisce that the company that had picked me as their first choicc a year back didn't even shortlist my CV now. He fact that T, with functional legs, the best firm on campus had wanted me and now I got placed with a firm that was considered to be, at best, mediocre, almost managed to dampen my spirits again.

Simi and I celebrated that night, with wine and a session of passionate making out. Since my accident, I had never dared to initiate contact with Simi, fearing failure, as the doctor had told me that lower body paralyses could lead to erratic sexual capabilities. Too afraid to discover the truth, stuck up bottling up my carnal desires, I had never expressed my urge to Simi, but I had to exit this sojourn someday and this was a day way too special for me, rather, us, to control my feelings.

One thing led to another and I found her turned on towards me. Of course, my attraction towards her was never a question, but after the accident, hers towards me was. She put to restall my doubtsas we made love that night: intense, rhythmic, and maybe since it was after six long months, but it seemed like a never-before experience.

A year down the line, Simi also managed to do an executive MBA and picked up a plush job at an MNC. Both well-settled, we lived like any other couple.

We gave birth to an angel of a girl four years into our marriage whom we named Vidushi. Simi quit her job to take care of the child and Hardik and I gave up our jobs to start our own venture, an apparel business. We figured a huge gap in the Indian apparel market, a gap between the expensive branded apparel and the local non-branded apparel, basically for the hep youth who want trendy clothes but at a cost which didn't hurt their pockets.

Initially skeptical of being a liability to the business because of my lack of my mobility, I was convinced by Hardik that I could do it, as he clearly demarcated the job descriptions. I handled all the paperwork and accounts and Hardik did the actual field-work.

We worked day in and day out and we saw the business flourish; within four years, we had three outlets in Delhi itself. The brand was named 'Spirit', a name thought by Hardik, maybe to always innately remind me that what mattered was the spirit to work and not my physical disability. To honour our love for cricket, we started a special cricket apparel range - 'The Spirit of Cricket.'

It ended up being a rage among the Indian youth and we, for the first time, fell short of stock within the first month of the stock rollout which was meant to be good for four months. There was no looking back after that as Spirit became a celebrated brand amongst youth, and 'The Spirit of Cricket' had catalysed this propulsion to fame.

❖ ❖ ❖

It is now twenty years since the day I lost both my legs to paralysis and, hereI conclude the most significant period, both in a positive and a negative way, of my life in the form of a short compilation.

I feel a little proud, to be the co-owner of an INR 10 crore firm, a husband to the most wonderful, loving wife on earth, a friend to the friend who meant more than a brother to me and a father to a doting daughter who now wants to become a cricketer and represent the Indian women's team some day. The dream her father once envisioned, the dream her father was once going to live, the dream that was cut short and made a mockery of by destiny, the dream her father wants her to fulfill.

Content, with no qualms with life anymore as I sit here in retrospect; though still jerking up from my sleep sometimes drenched in sweat, having dreamt of that light blue jersey, with GROVER written on the back in bold letters, as I take guard to a deafening crowd, incessantly chanting my name, and I, placing the ball perfectly through covers, sweetly timed enough to make it just trickle over the ropes and then take off my helmet to the crowd that erupts. I look up to the sky Gods, standing there in the middle, to the ovation as I lift both my arms to acknowledge the adulation that eluded me in reality.